"But are you certain you want a scandal?"

"Even when I have no idea what kind of scandal I want?"

He smiled then, a wicked smirk that made her overheated and trembling. Once again, here was the man she'd read about in the media. The bad boy they loved to write about.

"Luckily I'm an expert. I can guide you. How about one where you're protected? You'll look naive at the end, but you can walk away with your head held high. And you'll be untouchable."

"That sounds perfect. What are you planning?"

"An engagement."

She sat on the edge of the bed then, because the shock at his comment meant her legs couldn't be trusted to support her. "What?"

"Of convenience. Your parents seem to be worried you've fallen under my spell. Let's make it real. We'll say it was love at first sight and we're engaged. The press will lap up the story of a romance out of the ashes of your heartbreak. No one will try to take you away from me after that."

Behind the Palace Doors...

The secret life of royals!

Heavy is the head that wears the crown. It's a truth that Princess Lise, Duke Lance and King Alessandro know all too well... Whilst they might spend their days welcoming the world's diplomats and their nights at exclusive balls, that doesn't mean their lives are as picture-perfect as their royal images. Could having someone to share that responsibility with change *everything*?

To claim her crown, queen-to-be Lise must wed. The man she has to turn to is Rafe, the self-made billionaire who once made her believe in love...

Read Lise and Rafe's story in
The Marriage That Made Her Queen

To escape an arranged marriage, Sara needs the help of notorious playboy Lance. Their engagement may be fake, but their passion is no charade!

Read Lance and Sara's story in
Engaged to London's Wildest Billionaire

Both available now!

And look out for the final instalment,
Sandro and Victoria's story
Coming soon!

Kali Anthony

—

ENGAGED TO LONDON'S WILDEST BILLIONAIRE

HARLEQUIN

PRESENTS

PRESENTS

ISBN-13: 978-1-335-58433-5

Engaged to London's Wildest Billionaire

Harlequin Enterprises ULC
22 Adelaide St. West, 41st Floor
Toronto, Ontario M5H 4E3, Canada
www.Harlequin.com

Printed in U.S.A.

When **Kali Anthony** read her first romance novel at fourteen, she realized a few truths: there can never be too many happy endings and, one day, she would write them herself. After marrying her own tall, dark and handsome hero in a perfect friends-to-lovers romance, Kali took the plunge and penned her first story. Writing has been a love affair ever since. If she isn't battling her cat for access to the keyboard, you can find Kali playing dress-up in vintage clothes, gardening or bushwhacking with her husband and three children in the rain forests of South East Queensland.

Books by Kali Anthony

Harlequin Presents

Revelations of His Runaway Bride
Bound as His Business-Deal Bride
Off-Limits to the Crown Prince
Snowbound in His Billion-Dollar Bed

Behind the Palace Doors...

The Marriage That Made Her Queen

Visit the Author Profile page
at Harlequin.com.

To those who were told to settle, but instead waited for the person who could make them laugh and their heart sing. This story's for you.

CHAPTER ONE

'EARTH TO EARTH, ashes to ashes, dust to dust...'

Sara stood at the edge of the royal mausoleum as the priest intoned the committal service. A small group of mourners and official witnesses, as required by Lauritania's constitution, huddled round on a day that outside was too bright and beautiful to contemplate the three grand coffins of King, Queen and Crown Prince, waiting to be interred.

She paid little attention to the people around her, her focus entirely on the coffin holding the earthly remains of Crown Prince Ferdinand Betencourt. Their country's flag was draped over the top, bedecked with lilies, their scent cloying in the still morning air. A mere ten days ago she'd been Lady Sara Conrad, his fiancée. A woman one day destined to ascend the throne by his side...

The hysterical sound bubbled from her before she could stifle it. She clutched a handkerchief to her mouth to try and cover up the barely suppressed laugh at how foolish she'd been. She'd never believed ignorance could be bliss, but had learned a powerful lesson.

'You'll be by his side, you'll bear his heirs, but you'll never have his heart...'

Poisonous words whispered in a ballroom just a few months earlier. Words spoken by some woman, tall and elegant and worldly and everything Sara wasn't, telling her exactly where her place was in the hierarchy of Ferdinand's needs.

She frantically dabbed her eyes with a handkerchief, pretending her laugh was a grief-stricken sob. Had anyone noticed the sound of near hysterical disbelief? Because, in truth, she'd grieved the loss of Ferdinand months before his untimely death. The destruction of her immature dream that once they were married he might find the time to love her. She kept the handkerchief to her face, chancing a furtive glance at the assembled group. As she did so, a prickle of awareness tripped along her spine. She turned to her right and caught a man she didn't know staring at her. A stranger in the tiny band of familiar faces. She hadn't noticed him before in the throng of black-bedecked mourners and cronies at the funeral.

There was no missing him now.

He stood out. From his imposing height to the perfect cut of his dark suit and his undeniably authoritative presence. All screaming bespoke tailoring and old money. The only thing out of place was the expression of bored indifference on his face, while those around them were in the clutches of sorrow. A face that was square-jawed, cleft-chinned, sculpted perfection. His intense focus made her feel too small for her skin. As if she wanted to split from it, shed the dour black clothing she wore and morph into something brighter, more beautiful. *Changed.*

How inappropriate, considering she was supposed to be mourning her fiancé today. Yet there was no controlling how her body reacted to this captivating stranger. Much like she couldn't control the seething anger that twisted down to the pit of her soul—anger at the charade everyone had maintained around her. Perpetuating the vicious lie that she could ever have had a 'devoted' relationship with the Crown Prince. Theirs had been no growing love match, as she'd kidded herself to believe, but one of absolute indifference—on his part at least.

And then the stranger cocked his head and raised an eyebrow, the curve of his perfect mouth hitching in a way that said, *I see what you did.*

That look flashed over her, hot and potent. Petrol thrown onto the smouldering coals of her long-suppressed desires. She went up in flames, the heat roaring through her, incandescent and overwhelming. *He* knew she wasn't grieving like the rest of them. Her heart tangoed to an inexplicable thrilling beat in a way it had never done before.

Sara looked away before her lips quirked in return at his knowing look, which would have been highly improper and a complete disregard for her now worthless royal training.

Sometimes you knew things about yourself, and Sara knew she wouldn't have made a good Queen. It was no wonder Ferdinand couldn't love her. Not with all the 'unseemly' emotion that threatened to burst from her, which her parents, and the courtiers who'd been tasked with turning her into the perfect future monarch, had required her to ruthlessly contain.

'You need to try harder, Sara...' Their constant refrain at some misplaced smile or, heaven help her, laugh. All of them had seemed intent on squashing the joy right out of her.

They'd very nearly succeeded.

The same problem didn't appear to afflict her best friend, the only surviving immediate member of Lauritania's doomed royal family. Annalise stood across from her, expressionless, a slender, lonely figure. Did she suffer the same drowning sensation as she faced being Queen that Sara had experienced at the mere prospect of taking on the role? The frantic desire to escape the golden handcuffs of the palace?

Sara couldn't tell. The Lauritanian Queen was required to marry. Now, Annalise was unlikely to find the love match she'd once dreamed of. And yet there she stood, stoic and impassive, as a queen should. Not noticing Sara's inner turmoil at all.

Sara stared at the floor once more as she twisted the now tortured handkerchief in her hands, not willing to risk her friend seeing the ugly truth. That she'd been overcome by emotion, just not the one expected of her. Sara should be mourning the loss of her future, yet everything seemed lighter because she was…free. Of the expectations that had bound her for as long as she could remember.

She'd been betrothed to the Crown Prince at birth. Sara had known from the moment of first conscious thought that she was destined for one man, fated to be his Queen. Now, for the first time in her twenty-three years, her life was her own. Not tied to a person she'd come to learn was many things, but none of them what he seemed. It had been on the night of that ill-fated ball when she'd finally realised he would never love her. Any naïve hope that he could, quelled by his words when she'd confronted him. How he saw their forthcoming marriage as a duty to his country and nothing more. No promise of fidelity, just an expectation of long, lonely years trapped in a marriage without any feeling. Back then, there'd been no escaping the juggernaut of a royal wedding bearing down on her.

Now? Relief she shouldn't feel wrapped round her like a blanket. It made her a wicked, wicked person. Thinking of herself when her country's monarchy had almost been obliterated. Yet when had she ever had that luxury? Being a queen sounded nice when you were a little girl craving tiaras and ball gowns, until the reality of it hit like an avalanche. The relentless press, the jealousy of others, the absence of true friends. Till all you could foresee was a lonely future buried under the cold weight of expectation...

Still, that blistering sense of *awareness* hadn't lessened. She lifted her gaze once more. The man's eyes remained fixed on her, his mouth still holding its amused curve. A honeyed heat drizzled over her and she basked in it, the sensation new and illicit. What would it be like to kiss that mouth?

If another future had been hers, she might have been brave, done something about it. But as much as she craved to give in to it, such feelings screamed *danger*. Because powerful men like Ferdinand and this alluring stranger didn't really see women as individuals. She was more than a mere accessory, despite how she'd been treated when her engagement was formally announced. The sacrificial virgin for the royal dragon. The monarchical behemoth had threatened to swallow her alive the longer she'd stayed in its clutches. And she'd concluded that was all people saw for her future. To be a pretty little bauble on the Crown Prince's arm. To smile on cue, to bear equally pretty children and quietly fade into the background when not required.

No more.

She shut down her random musings. Turned away from yet another handsome man who made her dream of things that would remain better in fantasy than reality. Instead, she focused on her friend. Annalise walked forward to her family's coffins, yet as she reached them she looked at Sara. Eyes strained and weary. Mouth pinched and trembling from suppressed sobs. Tears forbidden to fall. Sara wished the world wasn't watching and she could console her friend rather than being required to stand remote from her Queen. And for a moment the weight of it all threatened to crush her.

Because they were both young women who'd lost the world they'd expected to wake up to each day. Their lives had changed for ever.

Sara bowed her head, saying a silent goodbye to the monarchy she'd thought she'd known but now realised she hadn't ever really understood. There was no fairy tale to be found here, no happy ending. Still, life was hers for the taking. All she could do was bide her time until her chance came. And now she had all the time in the world.

Lance loathed funerals. It wasn't the sadness that bothered him. Life was an unending parade of grief and lost chances. No. It was the hypocrisy. The exalted dead bearing little resemblance to the people they'd been in real life. The three individuals whose lives they'd been remembering today were that sort. Beloved of their people, but a mere fantasy. One he had no interest in remembering or promoting.

He'd been invited to be official witness to the interment, as the antiquated Lauritanian constitution required. Returning to the place of his blighted high school education during his father's long tenure as British Ambassador here. Lance supposed he should have felt privileged. His not so dearly departed dad had cultivated a close friendship with Lauritania's royal family, thinking it might assist his son's fortunes as the future Duke of Bedmore. But in truth Lance would never have returned to this conservative little country, even with a direct invitation from the Queen, had his best friend and business partner Rafe De Villiers not requested it.

He and Rafe had met at the prestigious Kings' Academy here, both fighting against the Lauritanian aristocracy in their own way. Those bleak years had forged an unassailable comradeship and a rule that if one asked for assistance the other would always answer the request without question. A promise made when they'd been abused at the school because they were 'other'.

Rafe for being a commoner. Lance because he wasn't *from here*.

So here he stood, sipping champagne at the wake surrounded by a dour sea of people. Tasked with reporting back to Rafe on the political machinations of the aristocracy because, as a commoner, his friend would never have been allowed to grace this hallowed occasion. Lance had no desire to reacquaint himself with these people, many of whom had tried to bully him at school, before he and Rafe had joined forces—and the other boys had realised they were a force to be reckoned with. It was a stultifying task, especially since a few of them tried to rewrite history and talk to him as if their past disdain didn't matter. Anyhow, his lineage was finer than the rest of them put together. Because inheriting a dukedom had some advantages, no matter how determined he was to squander them.

Still, being here pricked at Lance's keen senses. Rafe was up to something, hinting at a curious interest in the new Queen—a monarch who needed to find a husband, and quickly, as the constitution dictated. Right now, all the royal family's hangers-on were surrounding her with knives carefully sheathed, waiting to stab each other's backs at the earliest opportunity in a fight to be named King. He catalogued their names, the ones watching her with avarice, jockeying for an auspicious marriage. Some things never changed. Lauritania was steeped in the past. The future terrified the people here, and it was staring down at them with both barrels today.

Lance downed the dregs of his champagne and grabbed another frosted flute from a passing waiter. The young Queen, pretty as she was, held no interest for him other than an academic one. As his deliberately lazy gaze drifted over the room what he sought was something far more alluring. The flash of golden female brilliance he'd glimpsed earlier at the mausoleum.

Even swathed in black like the rest of them, she'd been impossible to miss. He supposed laughing at a funeral tended to draw people's attention, but it seemed no one else had noticed the well-covered slip. Lance hadn't been able to help himself. She'd stood out because she seemed so *unaffected* by the misery surrounding them. A diamond amongst these lumps of coal, and he adored bright, sparkly things that grabbed his attention and held. Only because in his life they were so very rare.

When he'd caught her eye she'd almost smiled. On a day when there was not a glimmer of hope to be had, she seemed filled to the brim with it. He'd sensed something a little wild and unbridled about her that in ordinary circumstances he'd like to get to know for a few hours in a large bed of tangled sheets. Or maybe the not so ordinary cir-cumstances were perfect…

Another glance across the room and he spied her, the bright beacon he'd been searching for, golden hair an unruly tangle under her black hat. He began to move, dodging the crush to get to her. Luckily, he was a head taller than most of them so it was hard for her to disappear even as she slipped in and out of the groups of people around her. He quickened his pace, his heart thumping hard at the pursuit. There was no way he'd let her escape him. The universe should allow him some small compensation for coming here.

She wasn't looking in his direction, staring somewhere into the crowd with a soft, almost questioning look on her face. Watching the throng of people circling about her as if she was some-how separate from the grief here. Yet for all the oppressive misery in the room, her back was ram-rod-straight and she held her head high as if the room was hers to own and rule.

A perfectly fitted conservative black dress skimmed her gentle curves, the skirt ending at the backs of her knees, showing off the swell of her calves. Her hair was pulled up from the back of her slender neck, curls drifting loose. Lance wanted to brush them away and drop his lips to the elegant sweep of pale skin at the junction of her shoulder. Skim his mouth along the warm flesh. See if he could get a smile out of her then. Or, even better, a gasp of pleasure.

Lance realised now, as he made his way closer, how small and delicate she was. Even in those modest heels she'd tuck neatly under his chin if he held her. He couldn't help thinking she'd be the perfect fit. As he reached her, he pitched his voice low, dropped his head and murmured for her ears alone, 'You've been a very bad girl.'

She whipped round, a flush of pink washing over her cheeks, a glorious wide-eyed beauty, too innocent for the jaded man he'd become.

He'd left the womb a cynic, his mother claimed. That wasn't *quite* right. He'd become an incurable cynic the day his parents sold off his sister, Victoria, to the highest bidder to further his father's career. Now, Lance's preference was for someone as world-weary as him. Not this fresh burst of perfection that made her little part of the room shine.

It was as if he were hypnotised, unable to take his eyes from her. Of course beautiful women were everywhere. He was a glutton for them and not known for his self-control. But he'd never met someone who made the room simply stop and melt away.

She tilted her head and looked up at him with huge blue eyes, so pale and cool they were like the spring meltwater from the mountains. Her mouth perfection in petal pink. She might have been the one blushing, but he was left speechless.

'And why is that?' Her voice was soft and musical, with the lilt of an accent that told him she was native Lauritanian.

No *I beg your pardon.* Or, perhaps, *Who the hell are you?* Because he was sure this woman had secrets and he wanted to mine them all. He saw it in the wide shock of her eyes—that someone might have seen what she was trying to hide. Her rosebud lips parted and she took in a shaky breath. God, how he wanted to kiss her. Right here and now. Might have been passable at a wedding reception. Grossly inappropriate at a wake. Though he'd spent most of his adult life being inappropriate. Disappointing his father had once been his greatest mission. Now the man was dead, but Lance still had a reputation to uphold.

And he hadn't answered her question. She raised her slender, pale eyebrows. As he closed in, he dropped his head again as if to impart something illicit. Then he caught the scent of her. Apples and blossom. So crisp and fresh he wanted to take a bite.

'You were trying not to laugh.'

The blush swept across her cheeks again. He'd been right. For her there was something about today that didn't match the grief of everyone else here. She placed an elegant, gloved hand to her chest.

'If true, that would have been incredibly improper of me.'

Lance loved that she didn't deny it. What a glorious mystery she was. Yet as she looked up at him tears shimmered in her eyes. Whilst he spent his life pretending not to be a gentleman, Lance still retained some manners. He whipped out a handkerchief and handed it to her.

He hated women's tears. Especially when there was not a damn thing he could do about them. She gave him a soft smile of thanks, took the sharply pressed linen and dabbed her eyes.

'Perhaps, but then I'm improper all the time, so I judge everyone by my own low standards. I always say if you can't laugh at something, life's no fun.' He was renowned in the press for taking very little seriously, which showed how underestimated he was. It was a carefully cultivated illusion on his part. Some things were deadly serious, like his sister's current circumstances. Everything else was simply unimportant.

The woman in front of him brightened a little then, a tiny quirk of her lips. He supposed he should introduce himself, but there was something about the mystery between them that carried an illicit kind of thrill.

Then she pursed her lips a fraction, blinking

with long lashes fanning her cheeks. 'You were at the interment. Should I know you?'

He put his hand to his chest and staggered back as if she'd mortally wounded him. 'Of course you should know who I am. Everybody does.'

No hint of a smile this time, but her eyes gleamed, their corners crinkling with amusement. Good. Better than the glittering tears threatening to mar her face. 'Lance Astill. My father was British Ambassador to Lauritania for many years. And you are?'

He held out his hand. She placed hers in his. It was so slender he felt he might crush it. Yet the delicate bones had a surprisingly firm grip. He turned her hand and bowed over it, although not allowing his lips to touch the smooth silk of her black gloves, no matter how much he wanted to. Today was all about games, and he loved to play. He stood back and released her, her eyes wide and mouth open in a tiny 'Oh' that could have been shock or surprise. At least there were no more tears.

'Sara Conrad.' The name sounded familiar. A Conrad boy at school had been one of his more persistent tormentors... 'I was the Crown Prince's fiancée.'

Lance froze. He'd known Ferdinand had become engaged to some aristocrat, but couldn't fathom it being this woman. She was too full of life to be squashed down by the strictures of the palace. And the Crown Prince was never known for his fidelity. Lance didn't imagine he'd have taken his marriage vows seriously.

'I'm so sorry,' he said. He wasn't. She'd had a fortuitous escape.

Sara looked up at him, a slight frown creasing her brow. 'Don't be. I'm not.' The words tumbled out of her. She raised a gloved hand to her mouth as if trying to shove the errant syllables back in, her eyes wide. 'I shouldn't have said that. Ignore me. I… It's the grief talking.'

He took her by the elbow and manoeuvred her towards a potted palm, out of earshot of most others. On the way he grabbed a glass of wine from a passing waiter. She needed fortifying. This woman was too open and honest. She'd be eaten alive by the crowd here, who gloried in each other's humiliation and loss, the bunch of them competitive to a fault. Right now, most of them were grappling to court the new Queen. This bright and beautiful woman in front of him would be a casualty along the way.

'You didn't appear particularly grief-stricken. Your laughter was somewhat of a giveaway…'

'It was hysteria more than anything.'

'You don't strike me as prone to hysterics. Should I have a vial of smelling salts handy in case you're overcome and swoon into me?'

The corners of her mouth trembled upwards and she sank her teeth into her lower lip as if trying to stop a smile breaking free. He wanted her to lose her inhibitions. To claim her errant smiles all for himself.

She glanced about the room as if searching for something or someone. 'Have you ever been in a situation where you realised everything you thought you knew was a lie?'

He looked into her smooth, now impassive face, fighting so hard not to show any trace of happiness. Yes. He knew exactly what she was talking about. He nodded.

She kept going. 'I was born to be a consort and look at me.' She waved her hands up and down her body. The wine in her glass sloshed about but didn't spill. She took a gulp and winced. 'Talking to some stranger, showing...*feelings*. There's nothing regal about me. I'm sure I would have been a disappointment. A terrible Queen. No wonder he...'

She bit her lip again, but not to halt a smile this time. Lance didn't need to be told who 'he' was. He'd bet his considerable fortune that the Crown Prince, and the rest of the aristocracy Lance loathed, had tried to crush the wings of this glorious being in front of him.

'Angel.' It suited her. She looked as if she should be adorning some classical artwork. Paint her perfect pale skin against the backdrop of a morning sky, with a pair of wings, and she could be a heavenly being to match any he'd ever seen on a fresco. 'I was born to be a duke and I've been disappointing them for years.' Her eyes widened and the tilt of her lips gave her an ethereal beauty that would have stopped everyone in the room, had anyone else been able to see them. Luckily, dark corners behind well placed potted plants were useful for concealment. 'The trick is, you need to own the role, not fight against it. You're untouchable if you don't care.'

'And you don't?'

Once, he'd cared too much. Not any more, not for years. Caring didn't matter when there were things he couldn't fix. Victoria bore the brunt of his greatest failing. Phone calls hurriedly ended when her husband arrived home. Strange bruises she claimed to have suffered because she was 'clumsy', when that had never been a problem which afflicted her in the past. The terrible suspicions he harboured, which had grown and grown in the years she'd been married. He shouldn't be trusted with any woman's happiness.

'All I care about is thrilling them in the tabloids.'

How they loved plastering him on the front page, each story more overblown than the last, when there was a mundane truth no one wanted to hear. Most of it was little more than fiction.

The smile on Sara's face was glorious and wide. *Unrestrained.* A warmth kindled in his chest. Better a smile than tears for a man he knew didn't deserve her. Now, if he could remove her hat, unleash her golden curls from the thick chignon at the base of her head. Brush the strands through his fingers. Stroke away her hurt and her fears until she flushed rosy with pleasure...

'You're a...a scoundrel.'

A reminder of who he truly was. He needed to stop his heated imaginings. Innocents had no place in his life. He tended to crush them with thoughtlessness. Victoria was his first victim. He didn't want there to be any others.

He bowed. 'At your service. The Astills are notorious for their vices.'

'Really?' The question was breathy and curious. Against all better judgement, he was glad that he'd piqued her interest.

'My forebears have spent centuries squandering our fortune. We come from a long line of drinkers, gamblers, adulterers and fornicators. I've a family history to live up to and I take my role as its current head seriously.'

'And in that illustrious list, what vices do you choose?'

'The marital bed is sacrosanct and safe from me. Otherwise, take your pick.'

Her sharp intake of breath made his heart rate spike. Her cool blue eyes twinkled with fascination. Lance dipped his head to her ear.

'Although of late gambling and drinking have lost their appeal.' His voice was a murmur, breath whispering along her neck. 'If I want to maintain the scandalous reputation of the Astill family, there's really only one choice left…'

Lance revelled in the wash of pink that once again tinted her face like sunrise over snow. A tremor shuddered through her. He moved closer. Couldn't help himself. Not that Lance would touch a woman so…untainted by life. But still, one could dream for a moment that things were different.

'Perhaps that's what I need,' her voice whispered, thick and breathy.

His heart pumped a bit harder. 'What?'

'My life…it's been so…' She fluttered her hand about again, as if trying to shake free the words.

'Controlled?' Which, in other circumstances, he would have enjoyed pursuing, especially when that careful control snapped in a torrent of passion…

'Yes. Perhaps a scandal would make things more interesting.'

She looked up at him as if he were the answer to every prayer. Very few people interested him.

Fewer held his attention. At the moment, this di-
minutive creature in front of him had him thrum-
ming like a tuning fork, all to her song. As if he
were the hero she searched for. It sounded as if
the beautiful Sara Conrad needed the fantasy of
an escape, even if he could never give her that.

'Oh, angel.'

Her pupils dilated. Wide, dark reflections of her
desires. All he saw in them was himself.

Lance's voice pitched even lower. Rough and
unrecognisable. 'Scandal I can do.'

Her lips parted. She licked them. 'Please.'

That one whispered word exploded to life. Left
him hard and aching. More like an untried boy
than a man who'd been unashamedly sampling
beautiful women since his late teens. The power
of her request coursed through him like a drug.
Intoxicating. Addicting.

Temptation, thy name is Sara.

He should move away, yet here, cloistered from
the crowd, with unspoken desire thick and heady
around them, there was nowhere he'd rather be.
Lance was lost in a world centring on her.

'Sara!' Her back stiffened. Her head dropped.
Lance looked over at a pinched-looking older couple. They turned their sour attention to him. 'Who
are you?'

'I'm Astill, the Duke of Bedmore, but you
will call me Your Grace.' Lance stood to his full

height, towering over the couple as he glared down on them. 'And who the hell are you?'

Their eyes widened and that look he was so familiar with, the avarice of aristocracy, swept across their faces at the mention of his title. Mamas had been trying to marry their daughters off to him for years, to make a duchess out of them. This pair's interest would pass. They'd work out who he was soon enough. What he loathed, more than the people before him, was that Sara stood there, still and silent. It was as if all the life had been bled out of her.

'My parents, Count and Countess Conrad,' she said.

Her father spoke first. 'Why do you have our daughter sequestered behind this shrubbery?'

Lance did nothing bar raise an eyebrow. 'I would have thought it obvious, considering today was the funeral of her *fiancé*.' He hated having to pretend she was grieving that wastrel, but he'd protect Sara's reputation. It wasn't his to destroy. 'Lady Sara was overwrought. As a *gentleman*, it was my duty to assist her.'

Her mother simply stared at him. Then she narrowed her eyes. Ah, there it was. She knew.

'You.'

He smiled. The moment of recognition always amused him. As if standing too close to any woman would ruin her for ever.

'Lance Astill. You—you're the…the Debauched Duke.' The woman spat out the words. Lance was quite proud of the title coined by the tabloids, although he didn't think it was their most creative moniker. He didn't discourage the nicknames since they kept most people at a sensible distance.

'Frankly, I prefer the Dilettante Duke myself. But I own whatever name they give me.' He leaned forwards conspiratorially and gave a leering wink. 'Since it's mostly true.'

The pair blanched. Her father turned. 'Sara, come with us!'

The beautiful Sara had her head down, shoulders hunched and shaking. His handkerchief was firmly pressed to her mouth. She could be crying. But he didn't think so. If he wasn't much mistaken, she gave a delightful little snort of amusement.

'Now look what you've done,' he said. 'She's upset again. After all my valiant efforts.'

'You've done quite enough,' her mother said.

He raised an imperious eyebrow.

She hesitated. 'Your Grace.'

He took her capitulation as a win. Baiting blue-bloods was his favourite game, after all.

'As have you. Upsetting your daughter on this most terrible of days. You should take her home immediately, tuck her into bed with a warm cocoa.'

Sara coughed from behind her hand.

He lowered his voice conspiratorially. 'That's what *I'd* do.'

At the mention of a bed and Sara in the same breath, her father turned a ripe shade of puce. 'Come, Sara. We'll take our leave.'

Good. Get her away from the vultures who circled here. Though he doubted her parents were any better.

Lance turned to the glorious woman before him. 'Lady Sara?' The way he'd positioned himself meant her back was now to her parents. She removed the handkerchief. Tears of mirth smeared her cheeks, her eyes aglow. A perfect smile lit up her whole face.

Time simply stopped.

Lance took her hand in his. 'It's been a pleasure, although I'm sorry it's in such unfortunate circumstances. I hope we meet again...soon.' There was no chance of that. He rarely came to Lauritania and had little expectation of being invited to the new Queen's wedding. Still, he relished the small fantasy curling between them that a second meeting was inevitable. *Fated.*

She didn't remove her hand from his. The warmth of her fingers seeped through her glove. They were lingering too long and they both knew it. She curtsied deep and low, holding his gaze.

'The pleasure has likewise been mine. Thank you for your attentions, Your Grace.'

And, for the first time since inheriting it, he gloried in the sound of his wretched title spilling from someone's lips.

CHAPTER TWO

It was some cruel kind of irony that had Sara sitting at her new Queen's wedding reception some two months after the death of the Crown Prince. On a wedding day that had been marked as her own. Though the room didn't much feel like a wedding reception. Yes, there were flowers, grand table decorations and a cake, but this place held all the joy of the wake.

'That should have been you,' her mother whispered. True enough. Still, it was a heartless comment if her parents accepted the fantasy that she could be upset by today. That it wasn't her sitting at the bridal table with Ferdinand as her husband. But Sara had come to realise over the past weeks that they really didn't consider her thoughts much at all.

'Well, Mother, it's not.'

'They could at least have made fresh choices. This was all meant to be yours,' her mother hissed.

No. This had never been for her, she knew it now. She'd fooled herself for years, despite the niggling doubts that perhaps this wasn't what she wanted for herself. The flowers in the centrepiece of the tables were exquisite hothouse orchids, which hadn't been her choice, but the most expensive and fitting for a royal wedding, or so the planner had dictated. The cake was a ten-tier monolith of baked engineering and fondant icing. She recognised it all because none of what had been ordered for her and Ferdinand's intended nuptials had been wasted, all recycled for Annalise's wedding.

Relief ran over her like a warm shower, though Sara wasn't sure it boded well for her best friend. The monarch who'd married a commoner, surprising everyone except Sara, because Annalise had mastered the art of quiet rebellion.

Unlike herself. She was a master of nothing, really. She didn't rebel at all. It was an alien concept. She was always behaving, doing what she'd been instructed to do. Even as a teen her only act approaching defiance was to grab a pair of scissors and hack her hair short in a fit of pique, a ridiculous thing to do because it had made her blonde curls tighten so she looked something akin to a dandelion. Not a great success, and in the end only made her feel foolish. In fact, she wondered what rebellion truly felt like. Was it a quiet thrill or something loud that got the blood coursing? Was it terrifying or exhilarating?

She glanced over at the top table. To the best man. The man whose white handkerchief embroidered with his initials was kept in the drawer beside her bed. A shiver ran through her. She'd never expected to see him again, whilst hoping against hope that she would. But he was sitting there in morning dress with a stern, aristocratic demeanour, the perfect tailoring of a silver waistcoat gripping his powerful chest, that torso accentuated by the best Italian superfine wool and Savile Row tailoring money could buy. He stared out at the crowd with a supercilious air, as if they should bow down before him. As if he was above them all. Her stomach swooped and her heart took off on a race of its own, throbbing as if it were fighting to escape from behind the ribs caging it in.

She might not be sure what rebellion felt like, but she knew what its name was.

Lance Astill.

Goosebumps raced over her skin at the memory of his murmured words, the caress of warm breath at her ear.

You've been a very bad girl.

Her toes curled whenever she thought about that moment, and it crept into her consciousness *often.* She'd fooled everyone else at the funeral. They all thought she'd been overcome by emotion at the loss of Ferdinand. A man who had never been hers to begin with.

Not Lance.

Because he understood. He'd owned her the moment he'd whispered those words in her ear.

He was rebellion all wrapped in a tall, muscular package with broad shoulders and narrow hips.

Ferdinand might have been born to be King, and he'd been an attractive man in his own way—God rest his soul. But Lance? She twisted the napkin in her lap.

He ruled the room absolutely, with no effort.

She'd watched people attempting to talk with him. Men, the young heirs to their father's titles. His contemporaries. He'd cut them all with a glance till they shrank away and he stood alone. The only one he spoke to was the new King, Rafe De Villiers. She'd heard her parents hissing that they were best friends. That together they'd bring the country into disrepute. They'd been wanton boys and worse adults. They had to be stopped.

All of that only made him *more* interesting. It had been bad enough googling him. But after she'd left the wake with her parents, Sara couldn't help herself. One tiny peek was all she'd allow herself. One illicit glimpse at that powerful body with defined muscles carved by the hand of a generous creator, as Lance stood slick and wet from a swim on the deck of some yacht in the Riviera. Or the action shot of him on horseback, powerful thighs gripping a polo pony as he was snapped mid-swing. The tremble in her fingers as she scrolled down the screen at the more salacious pictures. The scandalous headlines. The exquisite women.

It shouldn't have thrilled her. It shouldn't.

But it did.

Lance could teach her all about rebellion. He could teach her to be a *very bad girl*, and part of her coveted that with a secret desire she'd locked away deep inside of her.

But what was she doing, staring at him like a lovesick puppy? He hadn't looked at her, not once. It was no wonder, really. Her own fiancé had shown no interest. Lance Astill? She wasn't at all like the beauties who usually adorned his arm: tall, all slender limbs and perfectly tamed gleaming hair. The type of elegant, worldly women who wandered up to hopelessly naïve girls in ballrooms and told them what the world was really like, sending their carefully stitched-together fantasies crashing down. She could fool herself any way she liked, but the reality would remain the same.

You'll never have his heart.

She tore her eyes away from him. They sat at a table with people her parents knew from some of the older titled families here, where she was the only person under fifty. A few of them watched her with interest. Of course they might simply think she'd been staring at the top table, perhaps grieving over what they thought she'd lost.

As far as she was concerned she was the winner on this day.

'Look at her, wearing black,' her mother said, glaring at the top table once more. There were a few murmurs of assent. 'What was she thinking?'

The lack of respect for their new Queen shocked Sara. She ignored it. Her parents were obviously still smarting because their daughter wasn't sitting there now. As for the rest of the aristocracy at this table, she wasn't sure why any of it mattered. The world had changed and they needed to change with it. In Sara's view, the dress was a masterpiece of royal wedding finery, even if it wasn't virginal white. Sara mused that Annalise had given a lot of thought to the colour. Her choice was a devastating one.

'Her Majesty's been forced to marry when she's still in mourning. I think the colour is beautiful and respectful. Anyhow, *you're* wearing black.'

And so was she. It seemed fitting. Proper, even.

'That's different. It's her wedding day. She should be celebrating.'

'When her family has only lately been placed in a grave?'

Her mother crossed herself, then sniffed. 'She's Queen. Appearances must be maintained. And I thought at least you'd be bridesmaid. A deliberate slight. You would have done better.'

Sara was glad she wasn't bridesmaid. Then

she'd have to be next to Lance. Would have to dance with him when the time came. The thought of his arms around her, her body pressed up against all that height and hard muscle… She put her hand to her chest as her heart fluttered beneath it. Took a sip of water to cool the flame that had lit deep inside her at the mere thought.

That man was too much for her.

'I told you, it wasn't like that.' Annalise had believed too that Sara was upset. She'd told Sara she hadn't wanted her imagined grief paraded before the world. It wasn't a slight of any kind but an act of deep kindness and friendship.

Some music started, the lilting strains of a string ensemble. The Queen stood, and so did the rest of the room. Then Annalise and her husband walked to the dance floor and a waltz began. Sara loved the waltz, one of the many dances she'd learned during her royal training. The structure, the rise and fall of it.

'Don't worry,' her mother whispered, shrewd eyes on some unattractive man at another table as they all sat once more. 'Your time will come. Sooner than you may think.'

Sara didn't like the scheming tone. It set her heart beating fast in a way that wasn't at all pleasant. Instead, she indulged in watching the new King and Queen sweep across the dance floor, thanking the universe that it wasn't her at this moment, all the while wishing she was in another man's arms.

She turned away from the scene. There was nothing to be gained from hoping for things that would never be. She blinked back threatened tears as a shadow fell across her.

'Lady Sara.'

The low burr of that voice caressed like velvet over her skin. A woman who'd spent her life training to be Queen didn't fall off her chair. But Sara almost did, having to grip the seat of the elaborately swathed piece of furniture in tight fingers to steady herself.

Rebellion had found her.

The whole table turned towards Lance. He was glorious, his throbbing physical energy barely constrained by his formal dress. The height of aristocratic perfection. And when she looked at him she didn't see the barely tamed man he tried to present but someone swashbuckling, swinging from the rigging of ships, cutlass in hand, duelling at dawn or riding a joust. Her silly, childish fantasies getting her into trouble again, but right now she didn't care one little bit. He cast his gaze across the table, jaw hard, eyes narrowed in a look of disdain so singeing it was a wonder the people around him didn't simply self-immolate and shrivel to ashes.

Then he held out his hand, palm up.

'Would you care to dance?'

She stared at it for a moment as the whispers hissed around the table, her heart thumping in a frantic rhythm. All she could do was look up at him, at his stern face and quirked eyebrow, and grab this tiny moment for herself.

He tucked her arm in his own and led her to the dance floor, where the new Queen and King still seemed to be waging their own silent battle. Lance seemed to be fighting his own. Nothing about him was soft today. His jaw was hard, eyes scanning the crowd sharp as cut glass, a tension rippling through him that trembled through her too. He slipped his arm round her, she placed her hand on his shoulder, the heat of him burning into her palm through the layers of fine wool. It was enough to cause her first steps to falter, until the sheer force of him led her into the dance. And whilst all eyes should have been on the newly wed royals, they were on her. Like shards of glass spiking her skin. So she stiffened her spine, raised her head as she'd been trained to do and gave them something to talk about.

'You look beautiful,' Lance murmured. 'Although shouldn't you be out of mourning?'

His hold on her was relaxed. He moved as if he were born to dance, not a step out of place. The push and pull as he led her round the floor. She wanted to close her eyes, relax and allow him to sweep her away from this place.

'Isn't today supposed to be all about the bride?'

'You were meant to be the bride today,' he said through gritted teeth, but the look he gave her was full of concern as they spun across the floor. His sympathy almost undid her. The sense of loss, not for something she'd wanted but for the future she'd expected, almost overwhelming. Could he sense it?

Lance's arms firmed, holding her tighter, holding her together. She recognised that feeling. The pounding heart. The sick ache in her stomach. She'd always known where she was headed in life, never questioning it. Now, she had no idea what was in store for her, and she was afraid of what might come.

'How did you know?'

The papers could be cruel but most of them hadn't been gauche enough to mention it, too busy commemorating the new King and Queen to ask questions about her.

He nodded towards the new couple, a frown on his face. 'I have friends in high places.'

'You don't seem happy about the marriage,' she said.

He stiffened under her hands. 'I loathe any situation in which people are forced to do things out of duty rather than desire.'

'The press say it's a love match.'

Before her family's deaths, Annalise had confided in Sara that she had a secret admirer. She'd never told Sara his name, but Sara suspected it was the man to whom she was now married. The way he held her close as they danced, as if she were something precious, breakable, his eyes never leaving her face…

'How delightfully naïve. Tabloids lie. Or print what they're told to.'

She'd never expected he'd direct his air of disdain towards her, and found it stung. Still, she didn't need to meekly accept it. She'd accepted far too much without a fight. No longer.

'So the myriad stories about you are untrue?'

Lance raised a supercilious eyebrow. 'Checking up on me?'

The heat raced to her cheeks like an inferno as the corner of his perfect lips began to curl into a grin. She couldn't lie, she'd experienced enough of that in her short life. The unvarnished truth was far better.

'Perhaps…a little?'

'They tell exactly the right story about me. Disappointed?' Then his mouth broke into a wicked smile that caused a complicated dance in her belly.

'Thrilled.'

He laughed, a deep, throaty sound which rolled right through her in a glorious rumble.

Lance lifted his arm and twirled her in a perfectly executed spin that left her divinely light-headed. Or perhaps it was the man himself. Then he drew her close with an arm a touch lower than the polite height of her shoulder blade, his fingers splayed firm against the fabric of her dress.

'And what else have you learned about me through your avid investigations?'

That he had the body of a god, the face of an angel and the reputation of a tomcat. She couldn't help wanting to know *all* of him.

'Is there anything else to know, other than the apparent truth of what they tell?'

A look flashed across his face, a tightness around his eyes, and then it slid away as he twirled her in a giddy dance across the floor, the chandelier sparkling above her. In his arms she felt more of a queen than she'd ever done when she really had a chance of being one.

'You seem to have my measure, then,' he said. She couldn't miss the hollow, flat sound of the words.

She wasn't sure of it at all. The man was known as a rake, and if that were true he should have been whisking her off into a darkened alcove. Yet all he'd ever been was kind, which in her world was something novel.

Lance looked over her head, at the watching crowd. 'Want to give that lot something to talk about?' he asked, and she nodded. Then his hand slid down low on her waist, an impolite position for the polite company of a Lauritanian royal ballroom. His arm tightened and dragged her against him. The air pushed out of her with an 'oof'.

He held her tight against his rock-hard body. The murmur of the crowd grew louder as the strains of the music changed to something slower. A rumba beat, her dance teacher would have said. *A dance that represents desire and yearning between partners.* She couldn't comprehend why she should learn it at the time. If her parents had known, they would have thought it the height of scandal. But her dance teacher, preparing her for ballrooms across the world and many dances with a king, had told her that one day she'd understand. She lost the sultry rhythm and stumbled a step.

Lance dropped his mouth to her ear. A whisper of breath across her throat washed goosebumps over her. 'Let me lead you.'

Sara shouldn't, but she *wanted*. Craved the promise in his voice. Craved to melt into him.

Then he moved, and *how* he moved with her. As if they were created for one another. She let him take her, only a sliver of air between them, yet it was as if they were one person. The sublime push and pull as her body did everything his wanted, so perfectly in tune her mind blanked to all else bar him. The hiss of the crowd, the cloying scent of perfumes mixed with orchids. It all melted into the distant background as she concentrated on how they danced together, the heat of his body against hers. She felt dizzy in that joyous way she had when as a child she'd been allowed one ride on a carousel.

Lance looked down on her intently and the... *want* in his gaze froze the breath in her lungs. She could bathe in that look because it made her feel as if she were the only woman left in the world. She knew then that she was glimpsing the man the tabloids loved to hate.

And she finally understood what her dance teacher had talked about. Yearning and desire. The beating pulse of it, the ache deep at her core for things that couldn't be. It almost undid her in front of a crowd of hundreds. Sara sensed a movement next to them, an intrusion, and that glorious spell cast over her by the sinuous sway of their bodies faltered.

'Lady Sara, may I have the pleasure?' A voice she didn't know, the man she'd seen at the other table. She didn't want to leave this dance, the breathless sensation of being in Lance's arms. And Lance didn't relinquish her. He looked down at the stranger, all authority and menace.

'No.' A tremor ran through her as he swept her away in a turn, leaving the man standing on the floor alone. 'Unless you want to, of course.

But I thought I might save you a trying time. He looked dull.'

'Thank you.' Sadly, the space had increased between them to something eminently more respectable. 'My hero.'

'That's something I have never been accused of.'

The music changed again. More people joined the floor as he led her away, snatching two drinks from a passing waiter and handing one to her. She took a sip of the cold beverage with perfect bubbles.

'So what do you do when not being rakish or heroic?' she asked. She had to regain her equilibrium where Lance Astill was concerned or she'd dissolve here in front of him out of heat and *need*.

He raised an eyebrow. 'I'm a duke. That's usually enough for most people.'

She looked around the room. All eyes were on her, full of avarice and intrigue. A place she'd never really fitted in, she realised now. How could she ever have thought she did? They'd probably be chattering about her for days. She'd never liked the attention before, but now she relished the sly glances.

'I'm a little over the aristocracy and their intrigues.'

'A woman after my own heart.'

She shrugged. 'I just think there's more to

Lance Astill than...' she waved her hand up and down in front of him, signalling his clothes and general appearance of wicked perfection '...this.'

Lance's face was inscrutable as he regarded her, then his head cocked the tiniest fraction.

'I'm a second-hand dealer. Or at least that's what my dear old dad used to call me.'

The champagne caught in Sara's throat and she started coughing, her eyes watering. How mortifying, but she hadn't expected him to say *that*, even though she'd suspected there was more to the man than the image he portrayed.

'And yours was his *exact* reaction when I told my father my plans. He couldn't abide any sort of trade. Thought being a duke should have been enough. Though I did enjoy meeting his exceptionally low expectations of me.' Lance reached round and patted her firmly on the back to settle her coughing. 'Are you all right or are you going to expire on me here in the corner from shock? I'd hate to add that to my scandalous résumé.'

'I'm fine,' she said, her voice a little hoarse. She collected herself, wiped at her eyes, thankful for the waterproof mascara she'd worn today. 'Ignore what your father called you. What do you call yourself?'

He reached into the front inside pocket of his suit and handed her a fine white card, elegantly embossed in gold: *Astill's Auctions*. She cradled it in her palm.

'He loathed me using the family name. If he could have disinherited me, he would have.'

'That seems harsh.'

'He claimed I was a stain on the title of Bedmore, conveniently forgetting our wicked ancestors. But I'm the heir, no matter how disappointing. In the end, the dukedom won, as it always does. Anyhow, I told him I was merely refilling the family coffers, what with all the gamblers in our history happily emptying them.'

'What do you auction?'

'The possessions of the rich and recently deceased. They seem to trust one of their own coming into their homes and poking about their secrets, especially if death duties start biting at the family heels. Luckily, most of them have no idea what treasures their attics and dusty corners are hiding, which is where I come in. It's all rather grubby, but I'm the soul of discretion there at least.'

She couldn't see it as grubby. She saw him as before, a swashbuckling figure swooping into their homes. A pirate, definitely a pirate with his good looks and swagger, looking for treasure. What had this man seen in all the times he'd searched grand manors?

Sara loved beautiful old things. The lure of

finding some dusty object that turned out to be an item of value. On the rare occasion she shoved a hat on her head and sneaked away, she would haunt the Morenburg antique markets to see what she could discover. Her excuse was that she'd been encouraged by her tutor to hone her skills. For her, it was the excitement of the chase.

'Have you ever found anything incredible?'

'Perhaps.' A fire lit in his eyes, and the cold containment of him was dispelled again. 'However, it's a secret.'

An expectant silence stretched between them.

'I won't tell. Don't make me wait.'

Lance's mouth curved into a sly smile. Then he lowered his head towards her and her breath caught.

'It's *all* about the thrill of waiting, angel,' he murmured. They stood close again, bodies a whisper away from each other, 'That's what makes anticipation such fun.'

Everything slowed. She looked up at him, deep into his hazel eyes flecked with gold, the pupils dark with intent. All his attention was focused on her, the moment sparking with a kind of magic. Then he took a small step back and a long swig of his champagne, and whatever was between them faded like morning mist in the sunshine.

'I'm sorry to disappoint,' Lance went on. 'What I've found requires authentication first. But when it is it'll set the art world alight and make my auction house notorious. One more thing for my father to roll over in his grave about.'

She wanted him close. She wanted secrets between them. She wanted to…hold onto this sensation that shivered through her, one she had trouble understanding.

'You know the palace has a Michelangelo,' Sara said. 'Or so it's claimed. I don't think it's real.'

'It's not. It was painted by one of his students. But they like to pretend. How did you know?'

'I know the difference between a Rembrandt and a Rubens.'

Lance raised his eyebrows. 'I should hope so, they're entirely different eras.'

She rolled her eyes. 'I was going for the alliteration.'

He smiled again. The wry curve of his lip was back. The wicked gleam in his eyes speared her and she felt the heated stab of it right down to the tip of her toes.

'Still hasn't answered my question,' he said. 'Or do you enjoy…punishing me by keeping me in suspense?'

She could keep him languishing for hours if it would keep them like this, together, for a little longer. In the end she took pity on him.

'I studied fine arts. I wanted to help curate the palace's collection when I was…' *Queen.* Her tutor had thought she had an aptitude for it, an innate ability to pick real from fake. Something she wouldn't need now. Now, she had nothing. It was as if she were a blank notebook, yet she didn't know what she wanted to write inside. She had no idea what to do with herself any more. Initially that sensation of being adrift was freeing. Now, her lack of purpose and whatever new plans her parents were hinting at for her sat like curdled milk in her belly... She shook the feeling off. She had here. She had now. And she'd live in this precious and perfect moment.

'Anyhow,' she said, 'I wanted to do something useful. Something I loved.'

Lance gazed down on her in a way she had never seen Ferdinand look at her. Her former fiancé had been all cool reserve and disinterest. Now, she was being observed as if she were some precious bejewelled thing this man wanted to pluck from a shelf, lock in a vault and keep to himself.

'Who'd have thought in this godforsaken country I'd find someone like you?'

There was some movement to the side and Lance turned his head. She didn't take her eyes from him. She couldn't. His profile, the perfect straight nose. Transfixed by the curve of his lips. His strong, angular jaw. She noticed then a thin white line just under his ear.

'You have a scar.'

His head whipped round, his eyes widening a fraction before his lips thinned. 'Don't we all?'

She shook her head. 'No. Here...'

Sara couldn't help it. She reached out to touch and he jerked away. Foolish girl. Those unseemly emotions had run away with her again. This, between them, meant nothing. It was a dalliance for him before he returned to the UK and forgot all about her.

You'll never have his heart...

That was fine. She could accept a man like Lance wouldn't really be interested in her. Anyhow, after her crushing engagement to the Crown Prince she didn't need some dashing duke in her life. She needed to find herself, find her way. Flirtation might be on the agenda. Attaching herself to another man like a limpet, only to have him prise her off? No way.

Sara took a deep breath. She should go, back to that stultifying table with her parents. She was about to step away when Lance moved first.

'I think we've done enough to ensure you're talked about for a while.'

She looked up at him and his expression now conveyed the same polite disinterest Ferdinand's had. She didn't know why the realisation hurt so much. She had no claim on Lance. She didn't really know him at all.

'That's a good thing?' she asked.

'You wanted scandal. This is as much as I can do for you. And now I should take my leave.' He turned his head again and she saw there was movement at the bridal table. 'The King and Queen appear done, and I won't keep royalty waiting.'

Lance clasped his hands behind his back and gave her a small bow. Then he turned and walked away, leaving her clutching his business card in her hand.

CHAPTER THREE

LANCE WALKED THROUGH the cobbled back lanes of Morenburg old town. One more night here in Lauritania's capital and he'd be gone. He'd done his duty. He'd wished Rafe felicitations in his marriage but any hopes for his future happiness were a fiction.

Acid burned in his gut. Rafe was now one of them. Part of the Lauritanian aristocracy that had scorned them for years, though in the end Lance had sought their disapprobation. He supposed he couldn't fault his friend's choices. The chance to be a king didn't come round every day. Rafe had been on a quest for power even when they'd been teenagers. It had driven him to become almost the richest man in Europe. Still, that hadn't seemed to gain him the acceptance he craved. Not when the near feudal nature of this society was so ingrained.

Lance didn't care about acceptance. He'd tried once, but being the black sheep suited him better. His father might have fought to change the tide, but that man's respectability had only been surface-deep. Scratch it and he'd been as tarnished as the rest of them. He'd been mad for power too, would have done anything to ensure his family's fortune, his own career, even at the expense of his daughter. Vic had been shunted from boarding school to boarding school, whilst Lance had been dragged along to learn lessons from his father on politics, diplomacy and being 'a man'.

His father had once aspired to be prime minister. He'd never attained that lofty office, the family's chequered past not completely rehabilitated in his lifetime. In Lance, his father had hoped that dream would come true. As heir, Lance might have played along…until his parents had shown the contempt they truly had for their children's choices. He'd refused to engage with their machinations when pushed in the direction of a young woman his parents thought would kick-start a political career with an excellent wife from the right family. In truth, he'd been too interested in sampling the delights of many women rather than settling down with one for a career he wasn't sure he wanted. And, since he hadn't done his duty, Victoria had been forced into marriage.

He knew she'd done it to gain their approval. The girl who'd always been left behind whilst the family travelled for his father's postings. Searching for love and acceptance from people who didn't really see her value. He knew she'd attempted to buy those by agreeing to marry the man her parents had chosen for her. When Lance hadn't tried hard enough to stop her she'd promised things would be okay, that it was what she wanted.

But the deepest, darkest truth was that her marriage had got his parents off his back. The price she'd paid for his failings had been too high. The way she'd seemed to diminish over the years, from a vibrant young woman to something...*less*. Wilting under her husband's constant criticism, packaged as loving care. Lance's deepest fear was that the hurt wasn't only emotional.

That had set him on this path of destruction he so relished. Lance had gloried in his father's disappointment right up to the day the man had died. Even now he was mouldering in the family crypt, Lance hoped he didn't rest easy. Not after what he'd done to Victoria. The life she now lived. The bitter person who had replaced the hopeful young woman she'd once been. How he'd failed her was a wound that would never heal. As a child she'd adored him, followed him round whenever they'd been together. She would look at him as if he were some kind of hero when he'd tried to teach her how to fence or fly-fish.

He kicked at the ground with his foot as he walked, the anger always on a low simmer deep inside. This country brought back those thoughts—dark ones with no light in them. It made him far too introspective for his liking.

Except there was a flash of light here. A golden-haired angel who fitted in his arms as if she'd been made for him. He'd never really enjoyed dancing. He knew how to dance properly, because that had been expected of him, but he'd never seen the point of it when what he was really after was the main game of a woman horizontal. Until the reception last night, when what had started as thumbing his nose at the parents who'd turned her skin pale at the wake morphed into something else entirely. She was a woman to whom his body moulded seamlessly. He'd relished the light resting of her hand on his shoulder, the delicate grip of her other in his palm. Her slender waist and the way they moved together so perfectly. The time he'd spent with her had been more erotic fully clothed than anything he'd ever done naked.

Damn if he wasn't getting hard thinking about it. The lust washed away his bitterness and anger, replacing it with a thrum of anticipation he couldn't deny. If she were anyone else he might have stayed, sought her out and explored the blistering attraction, purely chemical and delectably rare. He knew she felt it too, from her dilated pupils and short breaths when he'd held her close, all soft and pliant as they moved together. They'd talked about the thrill of waiting. Of anticipation… All of that coursed, rich and heavy, through him. He could show her everything, hold her on a delicious edge for hours till she panted his name. But she was too innocent and *never* for him. She deserved a knight in shining armour. Not a wastrel. She'd already been engaged to one of those.

He exited the back streets into the bright autumn light of the main square with its emerald grass and flower gardens and fountains, making his way to the Hotel Grande Morenburg, its opulent sandstone façade dominating the street. As he did so, his phone vibrated in his pocket. He drew it out. The call was from his long-standing and, some might say, long-suffering butler.

'Is there a problem, George?'

Most of the time his estate and business interests ran smoothly, his trusted staff knowing exactly what he required and carrying out his wishes without question.

'Sir, the Snow family's rent is in arrears. Your agent is talking eviction. I thought you'd wish to know.'

Lance stalked into the hotel foyer through glass doors held open for him by gloved doormen who bowed as he passed.

'Mr Snow's unwell again?'

The family had been residents of the village for generations, proud people who didn't ask for help, even when they needed it.

'Yes, sir. In hospital.'

'The family require rent relief, not eviction. Ensure my wishes are made explicit. If the agent doesn't like it, make discreet enquiries about finding a new one.'

'Of course. Are you returning to London tomorrow?'

'Yes. There's nothing here to stop me.'

Lance hung up. The hotel hadn't changed since his first time here in his teens. Still gleaming gold with cream marble and massive urns of flowers adorning the foyer, the hush of opulence cocooning everyone privileged enough to be able to walk through. Time stood still here, like most of the country.

Well, he moved forward relentlessly. Hell, he wasn't going to stop for anything or anyone. He strode to the lifts. One more day, that was all he had here. Then he was gone. Leaving Rafe to his wealth and power and Sara Conrad safely untouched.

Near the lifts he caught a shadow, lurking behind one of the lush potted palms strategically placed all around the foyer, giving this place the illusion of an oasis away from the masses outside. A small figure all in black. Whilst he wasn't a stranger to illicit assignations, it was uncommon for him to find a woman loitering behind a plant in a foyer. But this alluring figure…a glimpse of golden curls escaping from under a black hat pulled low over her face... His heart kicked up a beat and his feet carried him to the palms in more of a hurry than his brain liked.

'Sara?'

She whipped round, her face pale and eyes wide as she seemed to falter and sway on her feet. He grabbed her elbow and steadied her. 'What are you doing here?'

She backed up against the wall, everything about her wound tight. That pulse of heat deep inside him started up again. The irrational flash of hope that her being here meant something. The curl of tightness in his gut making him crave to touch her skin, draw her close.

'I... I need to talk to you.'

Propositions were made to him all the time, business and erotic, by self-assured people as jaded and hungry as he was. They were always searching for something. That wasn't Sara, but part of him hoped, and feared in equal measure, that what she wanted was as dark and dirty as where his thoughts headed.

That she wanted *him*.

'Of course.' He motioned to gleaming French doors which led to the world-famous café where everyone who was anyone came to be seen. It was safer there—because the idea that they wanted one another had taken hold like a weed that couldn't be dug out. 'We can go—'

'No!' He didn't think she could get any paler, but somehow she had. Clutching an oversized bag close to her with whitened knuckles, her other hand curled tight into a fist. 'In private. Please.'

He held her gaze for a few heartbeats. It was impossible to tell what was going on behind those pale blue eyes of hers. But he knew fear when he saw it. The over-bright glitter of her gaze. A forced smile that wasn't for him, but for the world at large. There was nowhere private in this place to talk, and hiding behind a plant meant she didn't want to be seen. Really, there was only one option. Even if it started a pulse deep and low in his body, which he desperately fought to ignore.

'We can go to my room.'

Sara wilted a fraction, then straightened. Began walking to the lifts, all stiff and severe. He guided her to one, separate from the others. The gleaming gold doors whispered open and they walked inside. It was a small space—too small when she edged to the opposite corner and all he could smell were the flowers of some perfume he'd remember for ever as the scent of her. She slumped against the wall.

'The Presidential Suite?' she asked, her voice soft and lilting.

'It's always reserved for members of my family if we ever come here.' One of the benefits of being a friend of the deceased King. He loathed it, but still used it.

'Do you often?'

'No.' And he suspected after tomorrow he'd be here even less often than before.

The lift slid in a quiet rush to the top floor and the door opened with an elegant chime. Lance motioned for her to exit and slid his key card into the lock of a glossy white door, which released with a quiet click. He beckoned her in.

Sara walked ahead of him, through the parquetry entrance hall with its opulent vase of flowers, which didn't smell as delicious as her, towards an expanse of mullioned windows overlooking the old city. A view of tiled roofs swept down to Lake Morenburg, which sat in the middle of the scene like a livid blue inkblot staining the landscape, rimmed by the brooding Alps behind.

She stood at the panelled glass, staring out at the capital, the brilliant, bright day outside at odds with the gloomy dark clothing she wore. He hated that she appeared to still mourn a man who'd never deserved her.

'Would you like something? A drink? Coffee, perhaps?'

She shook her head then turned her back on the city and walked to the couch, falling onto it. Slid her bag from her shoulder and dropped it to the carpet with a thud. He wanted to go to her.

Instead, he stood behind an armchair with his fingers gripping the back, pressing into the fine brocade fabric. Far safer here as she took the hat from her head and placed it on the table in front of her.

Sara ran her fingers distractedly through her hair to tame the curls that now spilled around her shoulders. He didn't want to be standing behind a damned armchair. He wanted to walk over to her, bury his hands into that unruly tangle and drag her to him like some caveman who had no place in her life. He'd crush this fragile creature who looked as if she could grow wings and flutter away from it all. So he didn't move.

'What do you want to talk about?'

He tried for cool, impassive. It seemed to jolt her out of some sort of inertia. She sat forwards, picking some lint from her black coat.

'Scandal.' There was nothing cool or impassive about her words. She blurted them out a little too loud and a lot too breathy. 'You said you could do that and I need one.'

Those words stabbed like a blade. Of course she didn't really want *him*. Anyone could give her a scandal. He didn't know why that hurt. He'd never cared before. That sort of question usually had him leaping in feet first with indecent enthusiasm.

Lance moved to sit in the armchair to her right, at the head of the coffee table. He was up for many things, but he loathed being used. When he walked into anything it was with eyes wide open, usually as the instigator. He couldn't abide secrets and lies from someone who wouldn't say what she *really* wanted. He demanded honesty at all times.

'What sort of scandal?'

Her eyes widened a fraction. 'Pardon?'

He crossed his leg, slung one ankle over his knee and sprawled there, not taking his eyes from her. 'Do you need a tiny garden-variety scandal that will excite a few gossips over their afternoon tea and cake? Or a monstrous scandal that threatens to tear the fabric of your known universe and leave everyone ducking for cover?'

'Something…in between, I suppose.'

The flame burning in his gut flared a bit brighter and angrier. 'If you don't know what sort of scandal you want, I can't help you.'

She wasn't expecting that, he could tell. A small frown troubled her brow, her fingers restlessly smoothing over her dark trousers when she wouldn't look him in the eye.

Coward.

'Total ruin. Give me that.'

He gritted his teeth. He'd been thinking about the way she fitted in his arms, how she might feel the same, and she'd obviously been thinking about using him for her own mysterious ends. He wasn't sure why he found that so...disappointing.

'This isn't some bodice-ripper of a story you've pulled from under your bed, no matter what the tabloids say about me.'

She looked at him then, bold and bright, the Sara he'd dreamed she might be for real, rather than the woman she was showing him now—too much like the rest of them here in this abhorrent country. Wanting, expecting but not truly asking.

'I don't want my bodice ripped.'

At least she was prepared to tell him what she didn't want. Still. He leaned forwards, forearms on his knees, the curdle of disappointment rising in his throat. 'That tells me you have no idea what you're asking for. I'm no corruptor of innocents.'

'I'm not exactly innocent.'

He'd seen debauchery at its best and its worst. The aristocracy ran rife with it, and he'd partaken in plenty of the best. She didn't have a clue what she was talking about. He aimed to show her exactly how clueless she was, whilst she danced about him, playing games he detested.

'You either are or you aren't. There's no in-between. Some chaste kiss in a dark corner doesn't count.'

'It wasn't chaste. It was...' She looked at her hands, her fingernails. Anywhere bar at him. 'Moist.'

Which sounded like a hellish kiss, but a twist started in his gut nonetheless. She'd been engaged, but the thought of anyone kissing her… He didn't stop to question why the acid sensation felt a lot like jealousy. Anyhow, what did it matter? He'd made a rule long ago. Only deal with those as jaded and worldly as he was. He had no time or patience for anything else, no matter how tempting the package it was wrapped in.

'Chaste, moist…it's still only a kiss. Defiling virgins is not part of my repertoire.'

She looked at him then, eyes narrow and mouth pinched. She'd ignite tinder, the sparks flashing from her as she barely suppressed her anger.

'I don't know. It sounds like a fine addition to your business card. Purveyor of antiques, corruptor of innocents, defiler of virgins. Perfect for all you claim to be.' Slashes of red bled out over her cheeks. 'Except I'm not exactly a virgin, I suppose.'

Every person in this country would have expected Sara to enter her marriage to the Crown Prince a total innocent in all respects. Lance couldn't understand why the heat burned like lava in his gut, out of control and possessive. Still, he'd never show it. He leaned back in the chair as if he didn't care at all.

'No virgin sacrifice on the marriage bed, then. The Crown Prince would have been disappointed.'

The woman in question dropped her head again, as if she were embarrassed about the admission.

'He was.' She chewed her bottom lip almost hard enough to draw blood. 'He thought it would be a good idea to try before we married because… He said it would make the marriage night less…'

Lance clenched his fists. 'What a romantic. And did His Exalted Highness live up to all your expectations?'

He knew all about young women being forced into loveless marriages.

A shudder rippled through her. Her throat convulsed in a swallow.

'I had no expectations.' She held her head high and looked at him with bright, brimming eyes. 'Why are you being so cruel?'

Because he was furious. That she still hadn't asked him for what she truly desired, but seemed to think he was some kind of toy she could play with and discard. That a man who didn't deserve her had touched her, had made her first time awful, if her reaction was anything to go by, when it should have been world-ending.

The sooner he was out of this country with all its machinations, the better.

'Haven't you worked it out? I am who I am. Pick a descriptor. Despicable. Diabolical. I'm the Duke of them all.' Lance's jaw tightened. His hands clenched then relaxed. He stood and strode to a cabinet at the far side of the room—he needed a drink. It was past midday, so he wasn't being completely uncivilised. He grabbed a decanter and poured some whisky into a glass, tossing it down and relishing the burn. There was nothing more to be said. 'Go home, Sara.'

'No!' She launched herself from the couch and moved to the window again. Whipped round with her hair flailing about her shoulders, eyes wide. She looked exquisite. Untamed. Unattainable. Still innocent, no matter what she said about herself. He'd always adored a challenge, but she wasn't the challenge for him. 'I... I thought this would be easier. Being here. You're confusing me.'

A double shot of neat whisky so long after breakfast slid through his blood, but it wasn't the alcohol intoxicating him now. He stalked towards her.

'What about me confuses you?'

He didn't need her to answer. He knew exactly what she found confusing about him. It was written all over her. Her quickened breaths. Her eyes were wide, her lips parted, a pulse beating at the hollow of her neck. Something about it all made him reckless. Why *should* he care about her so much? She wanted a scandal. He could give it to her.

He reached out to all the spun-gold hair that fell around her shoulders. Took a thick curl and twisted it round his finger, before letting the gloriously silken strands slide free. He ached to plunge his hands into all that radiant hair. Tilt her head to his. Draw her close and kiss her like he'd wanted to from the moment she'd come into his arms on the dance floor. From the moment he'd seen her at the funeral, if he was being truthful. And he could show her many things. Obliterate any stuttering memory of awful sex with some bastard of a prince until the only word on her lips was the sigh of his name as she came again and again. Who was he to deny himself?

So he slid his hand along her jaw, relished the quickening breaths, her parted lips. He'd have her. The sex would be superlative and give her every bit of the scandal she craved, evidenced by the dilation of her pupils in those meltwater-blue eyes. Except another truth shone out from them which made him stop and pull back, even though his body screamed at him to continue. A pleading look that told him she was searching for someone to save her, when he was no saviour—for anyone. He'd failed his first test long ago, and had continued to fail ever since. A woman like Sara should not trust herself to his care, trust him for *anything*.

Lance pulled away and Sara swayed on her feet. Those dark shadows under her eyes, which he'd been too distracted to notice before, were telling. Had she been kept awake, reliving that dance and craving something more, as he had? After all the worldly delights he'd sampled over the years, it was hard to imagine that one ridiculously chaste turn around a dance floor could make a jaded man like him hot under the collar, but it had nonetheless.

'You don't know what you're asking for,' he said, his voice rough. He cleared his throat. It was tempting to walk over and drown himself in more drink, but that had never been his poison of choice, no matter what the tabloids liked to write about him. Now, drowning himself in her... He shut his errant thoughts down.

'Yes, I do. My parents...' she took a deep breath, as if she were fortifying herself for something '... I suspect they want me to marry.'

He stilled. A vision of Victoria's face swam into his head. Pale as her bridal whites, walking down the cathedral aisle on her wedding day. A tense smile, her eyes moist, shot at him as she'd neared the altar. He'd made a half-hearted offer to bundle her into a car and drive her away. To ignore what their parents wanted. But he'd joked about it and she hadn't realised how serious he'd been. Then again, he'd also neglected to investigate the exalted man they'd chosen for her. If he'd asked even a few questions he'd have discovered her future husband was not someone who should be allowed near women. He'd failed to extricate her from a terrible situation, one he feared became worse as each blighted year passed. But no. None of this was his business. Attempt to help and he'd fail again. It was better that Sara stood up for herself.

'You've just escaped one marriage. They've tried that before. It ended in disaster. And you're still in mourning, if your black clothes are anything to go by.'

'That doesn't matter to them... Our dance. They said I was running wild, that what I did was disgraceful...'

Lance barked out a laugh. 'A dance—disgraceful? Your parents have no idea.' The hypocrisy of it, when they were happy to offer their daughter to all and sundry, was astonishing.

'They say I'm to work on the man's art collection but, from the way they keep hinting, I *know* it's more. And the man they want for me...he looks like a toad.' She glanced up at him in a shy kind of way from behind veiled lashes, reminding him of how truly innocent she was. 'You don't. You're not toad-like at all.'

That admission of hers, in that hesitant voice, sent a sinuous curl of desire through him once more. He ignored it, knowing no good would come of this. 'Maybe you'll turn him into a prince with a kiss.'

She crossed her arms and glared at him. 'That

only works with frogs. *Not* toads. And I don't want a *prince*.'

The words were left hanging in the air, unspoken. *I want you.* He ignored every inclination to give in to temptation.

'I don't see how a supposed scandal is going to help.'

'You know how it is here. People like him, they want someone above reproach. If I'm not… But look.' She ran over to her bag and rummaged around. Pulled out a large blue velvet box and opened it. Inside sat the exquisite amethysts and diamonds of an antique parure, the fat gemstones glittering in the natural light. 'I can pay you if you help me.'

Little shocked him, but this rendered him close to speechless. 'What the hell are you asking?' He'd never been offered payment before. It made him feel as grubby as he pretended to be. Lance grabbed the box from her and closed the lid. Thrust it back towards her. 'They're not part of the Crown Jewels, are they?'

Sara shook her head, took back her jewels. 'My twenty-first birthday present. But I don't wear the parure, since I loathe purple.'

'You loathe purple?' He snorted a mocking laugh. When he'd glimpsed her in the foyer he'd had high hopes, but now they'd descended into farce. 'I have money of my own. How do you think I'm in the Presidential Suite?'

She at least had the good grace to blush. 'I thought you said you needed to replenish the family coffers, what with all the gambling.'

He gritted his teeth. Hissed the words through them. 'My father quite successfully rehabilitated the Astill name and fortune…' through canny politics and beneficially marrying off his only daughter '…and I'm sure all our ancestors, rakes and wastrels as they were, are rolling in their graves in horror. I've come along to rectify his errors, not continue them. And I certainly don't take money from women for my services. I will not sleep with you.'

She looked up at him, her eyes big and bright with unshed tears. 'You won't help me?'

'No means no, even in Lauritania. I suggest you try using the word on your parents.'

'I have, once before. When I found out Ferdinand didn't love me.' Sara gave a shaky laugh. 'I'm not sure he even liked me. I told them and it didn't matter. All that mattered to them was me being Queen one day. The power they'd gain. And they want it now.'

'You're looking for a hero, Sara.' She wasn't his responsibility. He'd failed at caring for anything, cultivated by years of selfishness. 'I'm not that man. I never was.'

'I need to leave the country and I don't really have money of my own.' She bent down and picked up her bag. Placing her hat on her head, she asked, 'How much do you think the parure is worth?'

'For the complete set, about fifty thousand euros, give or take.'

'Then I'll sell it. I'm sure there's someone who'll take it.'

'A shark might, for a quarter of that.'

'I understand. I'll go.' She hitched the bag high on her shoulder. He didn't want her to leave. She couldn't stay. 'Thank you for your time, Your Grace.'

The words hung bitter in the air, mocking him, as she no doubt knew they would.

'Sara.'

She walked to the door, turned and looked up at him with brimming blue eyes. 'It's fine. I'm sure it'll be fine.'

It'll be fine, Lance. Victoria had said those words too, moments prior to agreeing to her engagement, which had been beneficial to everyone bar the woman herself. He should have done more to stop her. To convince her to ignore their parents and refuse. But Vic had been the good child. Sweet and kind…once. Full of life, riding her beloved horses and caring for any orphaned or abandoned creatures she found. But not now.

All the life and caring in her had bled away. She'd done what had been asked of her when Lance had refused a political marriage. And nothing about her life had been fine since.

Sara began to open the door. He had no doubt she'd say no to her parents. But what if that didn't change anything? If he read in the papers that she'd ended up with the toad she feared her parents wanted her to marry? Lance knew he'd never forgive himself.

He hadn't been able to save Victoria, but he could try to save another woman. Getting her out of the country would be easy, he had a private jet waiting for him at the airport. In the end, some small redemption might come from the golden-haired angel in front of him.

'Stay. Please.' He walked towards her and put his hand on the door above her head, gently closing it. Keeping her in. Hopefully keeping her safe. 'I'll help you get away.'

Sara slumped against the door. Lance stood perilously close, his hand above her head, crowding her. As he had when he'd stalked towards her with intent and cupped her cheek as if he was going to kiss her. She took a deep breath, overwhelmed by the warmth of his body. The scent of him. The hint of leather from his casual jacket, which still seemed to cling to his skin, and another scent, something earthy and intoxicating. She closed her eyes for a moment, wishing he'd drop his mouth to hers. Show her what a kiss could truly be like. But she didn't think she'd survive it. Not at the moment, when every cell in her body was exhausted. As if she could slide down the cool wood of the door and simply curl up on the floor.

Instead of doing that, she turned in the cage of his body and looked up at him. His eyes were searching her face. She sensed everything was fragile—this seeming truce, his agreement to help her. She wanted to ask why, after being so cruel to her, but she couldn't. If she said anything he might send her away again, and she couldn't go back.

'Thank you.' The words were soft and breathy, hardly sounding like hers at all because she almost couldn't get enough air with him so close.

He pushed away from her and walked over to the cabinet again. She felt as if all the light and warmth had been taken from her. She wanted it back.

'I'm having another drink.' He held up a glass, raised his eyebrows. He looked more casual today, in jeans that hung low on his narrow hips, a crisp white shirt moulding to the expanse of his muscular chest. The dark leather jacket made him look in some way almost…dangerous. 'Want one?'

Sara nodded, unable to say anything. She walked over to the couch and sank into it again.

Leaning back into the down-stuffed cushions, her eyelids felt heavy. If she closed them, she could sleep for a hundred years.

Lance strolled over to her calmly, with his long, swaggering gait. He looked so relaxed it was as if this sort of thing happened to him every day—being begged for assistance by damsels in distress. He handed her a glass with a long pour of amber fluid. She took it and sipped. The peaty taste burned her throat, making her cough, but she didn't care. This might numb all those feelings, and she wanted to feel numb, for a little while. Feelings were overrated.

Lance sprawled in the armchair opposite her. 'Why do you think your parents are planning another marriage for you?'

Sara toyed with the sparkling crystal tumbler. The reasons were many. She'd guessed her parents' coffers were running low. Paintings had mysteriously gone missing from walls, rooms looking a little bare as furniture disappeared. The hint that her engagement ring didn't need to go back to the royal vault, that it could stay with them. She wasn't a fool—she knew what that meant. She'd just never thought they'd sell her off. More than once, anyhow.

'Well, none of my parents' friends trust the Queen, and the King—'

'Oh, I know what they think of him.'

'But it's more. If I'd been Queen it would have given them the ultimate power and prestige. Opened even more doors. Now that's all gone. They're afraid of losing what they'd come to expect. And they can't afford to lose any more. They might say it's only a job they want me to take, a chance to finally use my art degree, but I *know* it's more. They made hints at the wedding. It's also the way that man looks at me. Like I'm a...' Sara shuddered again.

She was no fool. The man looked at her as if she were a smorgasbord and he was starving. As if he were *entitled* to her, talking about a long and bountiful future she didn't want and had no interest in.

'Who's your new intended?' Lance's voice was cold as a winter ice storm.

'Lord Scharf.'

He took a long slug of his drink. Raked a hand through his hair. 'The man's over forty.'

'I know.'

'You're right, he looks exactly like a toad. We can't have you marrying that. You deserve someone dashing.' Sara trembled. The liquid in her glass quivered. She took another sip, yet the shaking wouldn't stop. A slight crease formed between Lance's brows. 'Do you want a blanket?'

Sara wanted to curl up in something soft, and sleep. Instead she inclined her glass to him.

'This'll warm me up. And I don't need to marry anyone.'

She wanted to live her life on her own terms for once. Not be beholden to a man, to any person. She'd had enough of being compliant, of not speaking up, for a lifetime. All she wanted was room to be herself for a while. Deciding what she really wanted could come later.

'A woman after my own heart. What *do* you need?' Lance might have looked as if he were lounging in the chair, slouching in a masculine kind of way. Yet there was a tension about him, like a wildcat ready to spring.

What she needed was some fun and adventure. To experience more of the feeling she'd had when she'd danced with him. The thrill of doing things she shouldn't. Of not being perfect all the time. Taking a little for herself. Of having a *choice*, not being dictated to by others. Being held in the arms of a man who looked at her as if she were the centre of his universe. She needed *lots* of things. But she hadn't really prepared for any of them beyond finding Lance and convincing him to help her. All she'd really done was grab the parure as she'd fled the only home she'd ever known.

Here, she was weak, completely worn down and fragile from the years of having no real control over her life. She supposed she could go to the Queen to ask for help, but Annalise was newly married—and what could she say? *Your brother didn't love me and he was cheating on me. My parents didn't care. They want me to marry someone else.* Lise had only just buried her family. Sara wouldn't add to the complications in her friend's life, or to her grief.

She took a final sip of her drink. 'I need a place to…hide for a little while.'

Lance blew out a long breath and looked about the room, then to her oversized tote. 'Have you got another bag? Clothes?'

'No. I… I grabbed some…' her cheeks heated '…underwear.'

She'd not planned in the end, just snatched some things and fled.

He snorted a laugh. 'Thank God for clean underwear then. Well. Clothes we can—'

A knock sounded at the door. Sara leapt from her seat, her drink sloshing onto her hand. She placed the glass on the table, her heart pounding so hard it felt as if it could burst from her chest. No one should have access to the Presidential Suite other than staff at the hotel, and Lance hadn't called them for anything. The room also looked like housekeeping had already been. No breakfast plates left on the dining table in front of the windows. Everything in its place.

'They're looking for me.' Her breathing came

out in gasps, as if she couldn't get any air. They were here for her. She knew it.

'Why?'

He had no idea. Her days were diarised to the last second, and she was always trailed by someone. For a long time she hadn't left the house without an army of people knowing exactly where she was headed, ostensibly for protection, but after the Crown Prince had died she wasn't sure what the need was. She wasn't important any more.

'I always have security. Today I…left.' Without a word to anyone.

'Does anyone know you're here?'

'I asked for you at Reception.'

Lance rose from his chair, calm and slow. Took another long sip of his drink. Pinned her with a hard stare, pointing over her shoulder. 'Bedroom. That way. Take your things.'

His voice was low and authoritative. Too soft for someone outside the room to hear, but to her it screamed loud as a shout. That he seemed to believe what she said was telling.

She grabbed her coat, hat and bag and hurried out through a doorway, closing it behind her. Then she remembered she'd left her glass on the coffee table. She opened the door a crack. Perhaps she could get it. But the murmur of voices signalled it was too late.

She tried to slow her breathing, but it came

in thready gasps. She couldn't hear much, only snatches of words like *'value'* and *'jewels'*. *'No'* and *'search'*?

Sara backed away from the door without thinking. Her chest heaving, she scanned the room for somewhere to hide and spotted a closet. She wrenched open the door and backed inside, closing it after her. Dropping her bag to the floor. She shouldered through hangers and clothes. Slid down the back wall till she sat on the carpeted floor. Wrapped her arms round her legs and huddled as tight as she could make herself. Every sound was muffled in the darkness of the closet. She tried to tamp down the sick feeling burning in her throat, the fear that they'd find her and take her home. She swallowed. Lance was a duke. His father had been respected here. Whatever he said, they'd believe.

But what if he gave her up to avoid trouble? She hugged her knees even tighter. He wouldn't do that. Would he? The silence crushed her as she tried to curl into herself, make herself as small and insignificant as possible. To embrace in physical form how she'd felt for years, with nothing but the cocooning blackness around her and the slight sliver of light shining through the crack between the doors. Then she dropped her head onto her knees so she couldn't even see that. Waiting for what seemed so long. Too long…

Sara jerked her head up at the cool breeze of the door opening. Coat hangers scraped on the bar above her as two arms reached in and pushed them back.

'Oh, angel.' Lance leaned forwards and reached out his right hand. 'Come here.'

She placed her hand in his as he pulled her upwards and she threw herself into his muscular chest, one sob after another cracking the veneer she'd presented to the world. He wrapped his arms round her, drew her tight as she gripped the front of his shirt and held on, all that strength cradling her as she wept in his arms.

'It's okay,' he murmured, cradling the back of her head with his hand. 'They're gone now. I'll look after you.'

She felt safe for the first time in longer than she could remember. The sobs petered out to hiccups, and then to sniffs as Lance held her, whispering gentle words she couldn't make sense of, till she came back into herself. Relishing the comfort of being truly held, pressed against his hard, strong body, she became aware of her ragged breaths and how his hand stroked up and down her back, soothing her. She could stay here all day, but she lifted her head, looking into his concerned face. He loosened his arms then and she pulled back and wiped her face. His shirt was a crushed, damp mess.

'I'm sorry.' She reached out and began smoothing the creases in the previously pristine cotton. The taut curve of the muscles underneath distracted her, the tight nubs of his nipples as she brushed her hands over them. He put his hands over hers to still them and his nostrils flared.

'A shirt I can have laundered.' If only washing away what had hurt her was so easy. 'Are you all right now?' His voice sounded strangely rough.

She nodded, his body hot under her palms. She pulled her hands away and wrapped them round herself.

'They were looking for me?'

'Yes. But I gave them enough truth to make the lie believable.'

'Which was?'

'You came to ask for a valuation of a piece of jewellery you'd been given for your twenty-first birthday. I valued it, and you left. Told them you'd asked for suggestions for a few pawn shops in the city where you might be able to sell it. Hopefully they're on a wild goose chase.'

'Thank you.'

He frowned. 'They were persistent and came with a man who looked like personal security.'

She shivered. He walked towards her and took her by the arm, guiding her to the vast bed. 'Sit. Before you fall.'

She shook her head. 'I need to keep moving.

What if they look at the security cameras? They won't stop looking until they find me. I've brought trouble to your door.'

'Is your phone turned off?'

She nodded. 'When I left home.'

'Then keep it off. And you needn't worry. They'll believe me and, even if they don't, I enjoy trouble and loathe bullies. But are you certain you want a scandal?'

'Even when I have no idea what kind of scandal I want?'

He smiled then, a wicked smirk that made her overheated and trembling. Once again, here was the man she'd read about in the media. The bad boy they loved to write about.

'Luckily I'm an expert. I can guide you. How about one where you're protected? You'll look naïve at the end, but you can walk away with your head held high. And you'll be untouchable.'

'That sounds perfect. What are you planning?'

'An engagement.'

She sat on the edge of the bed then, because the shock at his comment meant her legs couldn't be trusted to support her. 'What?'

'Of convenience. Your parents seem to be worried you've fallen under my spell. Let's make it real. If we're pulled up here or at the airport, we'll say it was love at first sight and we're engaged. The press will lap up the story of a romance out of the ashes of your heartbreak. No one will try to take you away from me after that. Once you've found your feet, you can break the engagement off and give a tearful interview to the press.'

'Saying you had an affair?'

He frowned. 'No matter what the tabloids claim, I'd never be unfaithful. You could simply confirm I'm the wastrel they say I am. You'll look a little naïve and I'll look like the cad.'

'But you're not.'

'The press say I'm the Dastardly Duke.'

It was her turn to frown. She didn't care what the press thought of him really. She wondered what Lance thought of *himself*, though. 'In my opinion Dashing Duke would be a better description.'

He shrugged. 'Whatever the adjective, it solves a problem. I can appear suitably heartbroken for a while before returning to my old ways. What do you say? My jet's scheduled to fly out tomorrow morning. We can be in London by lunchtime, with the scandal well underway.'

It sounded thrilling, it was everything she'd been hoping for, except... She dropped her head to her hands and groaned.

'I'd like to say, *Let's go!* But I don't have my passport.'

'You have clean underwear but no means of escape.' He chuckled, the sound deep and throaty as it rumbled right through her. 'Well, I *have* been in stickier situations. Leave it with me. Since I happen to know Lauritania's King.'

CHAPTER FOUR

LANCE SAT BACK on one of the deep, comfortable seats of the jet, watching the sleeping form of Sara in front of him. She was lying still in her reclined chair, her chest rising and falling gently, her pale lashes fanning her cheeks. Rose-coloured lips were slightly parted. Her knees barely brushed his. At least the dark smudges under her eyes were halfway gone after she'd fallen exhausted into his bed the night before.

He'd been a gentleman for once and taken the couch. Lying back, he thought how delectable and fragile she'd looked wearing one of his shirts, since she'd brought nothing with her except clean underwear, which he steadfastly refused to think about any more, because visions of whether they were lace or plain, matching or contrasting, conservative or risqué had plagued his thoughts for most of the night. At least he'd had work to do, things to keep him occupied. Usually his escapades were unplanned adventures, where he relished the spontaneity. This type of scandal required planning, so he'd put his wakefulness to good use. He only hoped Sara would be pleased with his efforts.

Their escape in the morning, such as it was,

had gone smoothly. No one had questioned her as Sara had crept from the hotel to a waiting car whilst he checked out. The cloak-and-dagger nature of it had set his heart racing. Even for him, helping a damsel in distress flee a country was something new. Her passport was freshly minted and delivered early morning via special courier. Lance smiled. Knowing a king proved to have some benefits, even though Rafe had been somewhat chastened and mysteriously wandering about the palace cellars when Lance had arrived. There was a story there that one day he might try to discover, but not now. He had better things to turn his attention to. Putting a smile back on Sara's beautiful face was one of them.

She needed some joy, that was clear. If he still had a heart, finding her huddled in the cupboard behind his clothes would have broken it. As it was, all he could do for the woman in front of him was hold her as she sobbed. And wasn't he the bastard to relish the emotion that brought her into his arms again? Clutching at him as if he were the only thing keeping her afloat. All soft and sweet-smelling, like a flower garden. Then when she'd started petting him like a cat he'd wanted to purr under her fingers. Have her touch bare skin rather than a cursed shirt.

Those insidious thoughts burrowed deep and low. Enticing imaginings that would have had him undoing the top button on his shirt, had he been dressed more formally. As it was, Lance adjusted himself in his seat. The whole episode had been entirely innocent from her perspective. Nothing to get excited about, but still he anticipated the next moment when Sara might look at him as if he were her eternal saviour...

The seatbelt light flicked on with a chime. The flight attendant walked through to remind them to return their seat backs to the upright position as they prepared for landing. Sara opened bleary eyes, blinked a few times and stretched like a kitten in the sunshine.

'Almost there,' he said. She arched her arms back above her head, the sombre shirt she wore stretching tight over her breasts in a way that was far too distracting. He took a final mouthful of the champagne they'd been given to carry them through the three-hour flight. 'Are you ready for what's to come?'

'What's that?'

Perhaps he should simply have helped her escape the country and then let her go. But she still carried a pale, haunted look that spoke of her family's, and perhaps the world's, betrayal. He'd couldn't leave her to whatever wolves might lurk out there, wanting to take a bite of this pretty little lamb.

'The press. A fiancée's going to cause a certain

stir. I'm an avowed bachelor who doesn't want to do his ducal duty and breed.'

In a flash, he could see Sara's children. Little moppets with blonde curls and blue eyes, as angelic as her. He didn't know why that strange thought assailed him at that moment. Or why the vision of her cradling those beautiful children, the ones she deserved, left him feeling a little… wistful.

Sara wrapped her arms round her waist and stared out of the window as the pilot announced their descent. 'I'm used to the press.'

He wasn't sure she knew what she was letting herself in for, but he'd shield her from the worst of it for a little while. Before the storm truly took hold and they were ripped along in its maelstrom.

'There's no press like the tabloids in the UK. The Lauritanian media are collared and caged by comparison. At home they roam vicious and wild, free to write what they want, and they love writing about me.'

'I know. Your exploits are popular.' Something inside him stirred. He liked it that she'd researched him, but loathed what she might have found. Most of it was an exaggeration he did nothing to discourage, because it suited his purposes. Only the most cynical tried to get close to the Debauched Duke. 'Why a bachelor? No children? They seem like normal things to want for most people.'

Here was that hoary little chestnut which got some women stuck, no matter his brutal honesty with them. Convinced they could change him. He clenched his fists. Flexed his fingers. These were the questions he'd been asked by more than a few women who'd looked at him, pretending to be wide-eyed and innocent, when he could see the hopeful gleam shining in their eyes, revealing their desire to become the Duchess of Bedmore. Though Sara seemed to have lost any gleam altogether, sitting opposite him looking tired and washed out. Not at all hopeful. He suspected that her enquiry was guileless, with no hidden agenda.

'The world does not require any more Astills,' he said.

His father had wanted to make the name *great* again, and Lance was witness to where coveting greatness could lead. To his shame, in his early twenties, thoughts of his destiny and inheritance had been heady ones. Whilst he eschewed it now, when he'd left Lauritania and returned to England he'd caught up with friends like himself, with power and privilege, wielding it whichever way they wished. He hadn't been true to himself or the promises he and Rafe had made at school. He'd succumbed to the allure of wealth and the benefits of privilege. It had almost entirely corrupted him.

Until Victoria.

She'd suffered, being only a tool used along the

way to further his father's quest for reflected greatness—the true victim of his parents' schemes.
Now, it didn't matter that his father was dead. His
life's quest was to tear down what had been built
and toss the tiny pieces to the four winds.

'Why? Yours is one of the oldest families in the
country. You have a long history, some of it…ec-
centric. But doesn't that mean anything?'

He tugged at the cuffs of his shirt. He supposed
it was hard for her to understand after a life devoted to duty and expectation. He was the perfect person to show her. Still, the prick of what
he suspected was disapprobation stung. Lance
wasn't sure why. It wasn't as if he usually cared
what anyone thought.

'It means *nothing*. I've told you what a pack of
wastrels we all are. Remind me to take you to the
portrait gallery at Astill Hall and tell you some of
the stories. It'll make your hair curl.'

'I don't need my hair any curlier, thank you.'
Sara reached to her wrist and took a hair tie from
round it, restraining all those glorious strands.
The band left a slight mark on her pale skin. He
reached out to smooth it away, then stopped himself.

'I thought you said your father had rehabilitated
the family?' she asked.

Lance swallowed, to equalise the pressure in
his ears. With him not wanting children and Vic-

toria being unable to have them, no matter how hard she'd tried, the earth would be washed clean of their blood. There'd be nothing left *to* rehabilitate.

'Nothing can take away the stain of all those black sheep. The best thing to do is put us all out of our misery. But enough about me.' Their interactions weren't meant to be about deep and meaningful questions. For her, at least, it was about injecting some fun into her life—and he knew *all* about fun. Still, on that front, they had work to do. 'Our first job is to get you some clothes. Then we'll take the helicopter to Astill Hall.'

She'd like that. Shopping, then a sightseeing flight over London on their way to the country, keeping her away from the capital, where the worst of the tabloids lurked. At least in his ancestral home he could maintain some control and privacy. Hell knew when he'd become so considerate. It was an unfamiliar sensation.

Sara smoothed her hands over the exquisitely tailored but dreadful black trousers. He wanted to burn every black item of clothing she owned. Dress her in jewelled colours so she couldn't pretend to grieve any longer.

Sara shook her head. A rogue curl fell free over her face. She tucked it behind her ear.

'I don't have any money for shopping.'

'I do.' Lance shrugged. 'No fiancée of mine is

ever going to pay for her own things. It's one of the perks of being with me, even in a sham engagement.'

None of the women he'd been with who *weren't* his fiancée had complained about his generosity. In fact, they'd seemed ecstatic. He enjoyed making people happy, *especially* women. But Sara fixed him with a glare that would have slapped down even royalty.

'I need to sell the parure and I need a job.'

'If you really want to offload the jewels, they'll be taken care of today. As for work, you don't have the right visa, so that poses a problem. But you don't need a job immediately.'

'So you expect your fiancée to sit at home and take care of the manor?'

Strangely, that idea suddenly had boundless appeal. Someone there other than staff and the lonely halls, half of which he'd shut down because he didn't use them. A beautiful, smiling face welcoming him home, with little blonde cherubs running behind her when she opened the door to greet him as he...

An odd warmth ignited in his chest at the thought. He slammed those thoughts into the vault of his imagination.

'Of course not.' The damned champagne was addling his brain. He should have stuck to water.

'Then I need to do something.'

With her lack of experience and a fine arts degree, he suspected there weren't many places who would take her, *except*… 'You can work with me.'

'I can't take your clothes or your money!'

'You can't continue to wear what you're wearing now, since it's all you have.' The vision of her in one of his shirts the night before drifted lazily through his consciousness. It had swamped her. She'd looked impossibly alluring, scrubbed clean of make-up, all mussed up as if they'd just had… Once again he tried to shut down his errant imagination. When had it become so fertile? 'And if not money, didn't Ferdinand give you gifts?'

He didn't know why the words hissed out so vehemently.

'No. The only thing he ever gave me was the engagement ring.'

With all the Crown's riches, her fiancé should have draped her in gems, spread glittering trinkets over her flawless, naked flesh…

He *really* needed to stick to business.

'You won't be taking my money. You'll be earning it, in a way. Whilst I can't officially employ you, we can come to some sort of arrangement. I'm always looking for treasure. You might be able to help me find some.'

She sat up a bit straighter and a beaming smile broke out over her face, as beautiful as the first rays of sunshine spilling over the horizon. A man could be quite dazzled by her, if he allowed himself.

'I used to do that in the Morenburg markets.'

Undiscovered antiques were the only thing of worth in Lauritania, as far as he was concerned.

'Did you find any treasures?'

Sara cocked her head to the side, her eyes narrowed, the corner of her mouth curling till she looked quite sly.

'It's a…secret.'

He saw what she was doing. The thrill of it was like a lick of fire igniting in his belly. 'Don't keep me waiting.'

Sara put her finger to her lips and tapped, as if she were thinking. 'I seem to recall someone telling me it was *all* about the excitement of waiting.'

She thought to turn those tables on him? He chuckled. 'One day, angel, I'll truly teach you about waiting for what you crave. That'll be one hell of a lesson.'

Her face softened, and her mouth opened as if it was too hard to take in air. Her pupils flared, big and dark, in the pale blue of her eyes. She shifted in her seat as his words were left hanging in the air. What was he playing at? This game was about saving Sara, not seducing her.

'How about we make a deal?' he asked, wrestling the conversation back on track.

'O…okay?'

He tried to ignore her little stutter. The way the word came out all soft and hopeful.

'You tell me, and I'll tell you.'

She laughed and it seemed as if the whole day brightened around him again.

'It's not much, really. A miniature teapot in pristine condition, which I think is antique Meissen porcelain. My art history tutor was having it appraised. He believes it's quite rare.'

Whilst she said it wasn't much, Sara sat up straighter, her face alight, gaze distant as if she was recalling the moment she'd found it. He understood that electric sensation, discovering something others had forgotten about or didn't value.

'Well done,' he said. 'Highly collectible.'

She shrugged. 'It's impossibly pretty, and I was lucky.' Then she leaned forwards, hands clasped in front of her. 'Now it's your turn.'

'Remember, it's yet to be authenticated.' But it would be, he was certain of it. Lance leaned back in his chair, stretching the moment out, his heart beating a little faster even now, his recollection of that moment twelve months before when he'd unwrapped a filthy oilcloth and uncovered a masterpiece.

'A Caravaggio. Found it in someone's attic.'

Her eyes widened. *'No.'*

How he wanted to reach forwards, cup her face in his hands and brush his lips across hers. Take their mutual excitement and channel it into something messier and hotter. But Sara wasn't for him. She was looking at him as if he were some miracle when his life was littered with failings.

'Yes. And *when* it's authenticated it'll cause a huge stir.'

'But that's worth…'

'It's priceless.'

In so many ways. Most importantly, in creating an escape plan for his sister. She'd refused all offers of money to help her leave her husband, claiming it was somehow tainted. She wouldn't take anything from a fortune bestowed on him by the family that had hurt her so terribly. That meant any financial assistance he offered had to come from what he *earned* in his business. With the sale of the Caravaggio, he'd have proof that the funds had come from his work and not the family coffers. That painting was a way to help Vic, make her safe.

'I wish I could find something like that. It would feel amazing.' She was looking up at him in wonder now. As if he held the secrets of the universe. He wanted to keep that look on her face, even though he didn't deserve it.

'It did. Which brings me back to you and your need for finances. Help me, and if you locate anything of value I'll gift you the equivalent of the buyer's premium at auction when our arrangement ends. Fifteen percent.'

'I— What? Wait.' Sara held up her hands. 'You say you're buying my clothes. Now this? I can't take charity.'

'It's not charity. I own an auction house. I find hidden treasure and sell it. You have the right qualifications and want to find treasure too. It's perfect.'

She shook her head. Another golden corkscrew of hair tumbled free. She blew it out of her eyes. 'Even if I can't be an employee, I want to be paid as if I were.'

'I don't have another employee like you.'

'*Exactly.* It isn't a commercial arrangement. I… I'll take two percent.'

'Accepting that would be robbery on my part. I have the funds, why won't you take them?'

'I need to learn to look after myself. What about when we're not together? What then?'

Lance frowned. In these moments she sounded so much like Vic… Yet he understood pride. He needed to play smart here. He shrugged.

'I suspect it will cost me nothing, since you're unlikely to find anything of value at all. But if you're concerned…twelve percent.'

Sara's eyes narrowed, and her lips pursed. Ah, he had her now.

'Of *course* I'll find something. Five.'

'Ten.'

'Seven and a half. And that's *final*.'

It wasn't enough, but he'd give it to her. He sensed she needed a win of her own.

'You strike a hard deal, Lady Sara.' Lance held out his hand and she slipped her cool palm into his as they shook in agreement. He should let her go but marvelled at how it was the perfect fit. Their eyes met, palms locked between them. Her eyes widened.

Then the plane jolted with a bump on the tarmac and began taxiing to the terminal. She pulled her hand from his. He missed the warmth of her soft skin on his own. Craved it like some beacon in the darkness, when in truth the darkness was where he belonged.

Moments after they left the plane, everything had become a blur of activity. Sara's head still spun. After some short time to freshen up, they'd been collected by car to travel to London. She'd exchanged details with his secretary so she could sync Sara and Lance's diaries. When she briefly turned on her phone to check the coming days' events, multiple message alerts angrily pinged at her. She turned it off, dropping it into her bag.

Lance looked up from his phone, on which he'd been assiduously working, cocking one eyebrow. 'Trouble?'

Most of the messages had come from her parents and brother. But there was one from Annalise. Her family, she wouldn't deal with. Lise, she *couldn't*. How could she admit what was going on to her friend?

She shrugged. 'It's to be expected. Where are we going now?'

She and Lance had come to a kind of agreement about her clothes. He'd arranged for someone to meet them at Astill Hall that very afternoon and had handed over his phone so she could speak to a lovely woman who'd asked what she was looking for in terms of style. 'Economical and fun' was what Sara wanted. Lance had taken the phone and insisted that not an item of clothing was to be black. Sara didn't really care. He was paying, after all. But when her parure was sold, she'd pay him back. Anything else didn't seem right, especially when she needed to take care of herself.

The car began to slow, and then came to a stop. The chauffeur opened his door.

'Could you give us a few moments?' Lance asked.

The driver nodded and left the vehicle, standing close by.

'The minute we step out of this car, the game begins.' Lance's voice was low and steady, in some ways reassuring. And still her heart skipped a few beats.

'What game?'

His responding slow grin was pure wickedness. If it could be bottled, it would corrupt millions and send the world into chaos. 'The tabloid media—one of my favourite amusements. Are you ready to play?'

'Yes.'

He clapped his hands together. 'Excellent! Now, what's your favourite food? Not something ordinary. Your guilty pleasure.'

She looked at him, sitting there in a magnificent pinstriped suit and pristine sky-blue shirt. His hair gleamed like burnished gold. This man, *he* could become her guilty pleasure. It would be so easy to lose her head around him. But he didn't want her. He'd made that clear. It wasn't what he was asking for...

'Sacher torte.'

'Excellent choice. Now...' He nodded to the driver, who opened Lance's door. Lance hopped out and bent down to look at her. 'Look at me like you look at a slice of Sacher torte. You know you want it but shouldn't have it. It's decadent. It's *sinful*. You're going to eat it anyhow.'

She didn't know what to say. Her mouth dropped open, because the idea of thinking of him like that was now filling her brain. He frowned.

'You look like you've come down with indigestion.'

She shut her eyes. 'Okay. Right.' She took a deep breath, because she knew how to act. She'd spent a lifetime doing so. When she opened her eyes again she allowed herself to admire the tempting hint of chest where he wore no tie. Wondered how his skin would feel there. If she'd be able to feel the beat of his heart under her palm…

'Perfect. Just like that,' he murmured, his gaze softening. 'Good girl.'

The words made her feel like a *bad girl.* If a human being could self-combust, she would have lit up like a torch. She wasn't sure her legs would work right now. Everything about her simply melted.

He seemed to realise she needed a bit of help, reaching his hand into the car, palm up. She placed hers into it and he squeezed, then assisted her out. He slipped his arm round her waist and led her down a narrow, cobbled lane to a small midnight-blue door. The only sign on the premises was a name, John T Smith, in gleaming gold.

'What is this place?' she asked.

'Somewhere we can find a man who can help with your amethysts.'

'Is John Smith really his name?'

The corner of Lance's mouth curved up into a sly smile. 'I've never been impolite enough to ask.'

As he pushed the door open a little bell tinkled. They walked into the dimly lit room, which glittered with sparkling glass display cabinets full of gold, silver and porcelain. The walls were adorned with magnificent artworks in ancient gilded frames.

'Oh.' It was all she could say. She knew the value of some of the pieces here. It was an incredible collection of rare and valuable objects.

'Thought you'd appreciate it,' Lance murmured.

A man walked out from behind a curtain. He was wiry and small like a jockey, with a beaming smile for Lance.

'Your Grace, how good to see you again.' His voice sounded overly deferential, but he winked at Sara, and she smiled back at him.

'Cut it, John.'

'I'm trying to be properly polite to my betters.'

Lance sighed. 'When have you ever thought me better than you?'

'Never.' He turned his attention to Sara then. 'But this vision before me. She's better than the both of us combined.'

'She is indeed.' Lance squeezed her hand and introduced them. 'You know why we're here.'

'The parure. May I see it?'

Sara dug into her bag and handed over the box. The man behind the counter opened it. He pulled out a jeweller's eyeglass and began looking the piece over.

'Well, then.'

'You know my thoughts,' Lance said.

'I think you're a bit light on in your valuation. Losing your touch.' John Smith looked at Sara and frowned. 'This is a valuable suite of jewels and amethysts are all the rage at the moment. Are you sure you want to sell?'

She'd never been more certain in her life. 'Yes. How much do you think it's worth?'

'Well. Your fiancé here thinks it's worth fifty. I believe a bit more, but after buyer's premium you could get fifty-five.' He turned his attention to Lance. 'You're not going to auction it?'

'That wouldn't be proper.'

John narrowed his eyes at her. 'No, I'm guessing not. Want me to arrange things?'

'Please. Now, what else do you have for us?'

John took a bundle of tinkling keys from his belt and unlocked a drawer. 'A couple of items you might be interested in. Did you hear old Fothergill's dead?'

He fiddled with the drawer and pulled out two small satin bags.

'No,' Lance said. 'How's young Lady Fothergill coping?'

'She was in here the other day. Think things are tight in that big, lonely estate of hers. She was selling off some trinkets. I asked if she wanted you to call and she does. I can text you her number.'

'As always, thank you.'

'Now, here is what I was talking about.'

He pulled out a velvet-covered tray, opened the little pouches and spilled two glittering rings onto the inky surface.

Sara's heart stuttered, before beating a little faster. 'What's this?' she said as if her voice wasn't her own.

'If we're engaged, you need a ring.'

John smiled like the Cheshire cat. 'He told me all about you. Asked me for the most interesting ones I have. And here they are.'

He waved them over with a flourish. Lance picked up the first, an enormous sapphire the colour of worn denim, with tiny diamonds surrounding it. It was old, outstanding. He twirled it under the lights then picked up the other ring, which was smaller but no less beautiful. An oval opal which shone like a rainbow. Again, surrounded by diamonds with a carved gold band. The sapphire was magnificent, but the opal…

It took her breath away.

'This,' Lance murmured. She held her breath as he twisted it under the lights and it changed colour with every turn. 'Beautiful and complex, like you.'

He looked at her, in that second entirely inscrutable, unknowable. 'Let's see what it looks like in natural light.'

Lance took her hand again, the warm grasp of

it unusual, unnecessary, and it sent a shimmer of pleasure right through her. He led her out of the shop, the little bell tinkling its quaint tinny sound as they walked into the lane once more. A chill breeze blew as leaves skittered around them. Something about this felt…important. Far more significant than it all really was. And she didn't want to look at Lance, or the exquisite piece of jewellery he held. The morning had seemed fun, the fantasy of it all. But this was all too much, too real. She looked up at the grey sky, which always seemed to follow them here, and wrapped her coat a little more tightly round her.

'Autumn's coming earlier this year.'

Lance chuckled. 'I'm not out here to talk about the weather. Do you like it?'

He held out his hand, the ring pinched between his thumb and forefinger. She looked down at the exquisite opal, full of fire with pinks and greens and blues, the muted gleam of old cut diamonds framing the edge of the gemstone. It took her breath away, this ring. How could she not love everything about it? Still she shook her head.

'You prefer the sapphire?'

He'd compared the opal to her. *Beautiful and complex.* It had so much meaning. Too much, if she let her imagination run wild. 'Aren't opals supposed to be bad luck?'

'Only for the faithless, apparently. Which I suppose means I'm doomed.'

She looked up at him, staring down at her with earnest hazel eyes. 'You said you'd never be unfaithful.'

'That's true. Perhaps there's a meagre chance for me after all.' He chuckled. 'So, what do you think? Will it do?'

'It's too much. Surely you have something in some vault you could use?'

'The traditional engagement ring in my family would be the Astill Amethyst.' He smiled. 'You hate purple. If you don't like the opal, we can find something else.'

Something clenched deep inside her. Her parents hadn't remembered she hated purple when they'd presented her with the parure on her twenty-first birthday. Or perhaps they didn't care. She looked at the ring, still held between them by Lance's long, elegant fingers.

'It's perfect,' Sara whispered.

'Then it's yours.'

He slid the jewel into the pocket of his trousers and took her left hand. Lifted it to his lips and kissed. A flush of heat flooded her cheeks.

'There's really no need—'

'Hush.' He pulled her into him. Leaned down. This close, with all his vibrancy and vigour and strength, the man was too much. Sara closed her eyes, absorbing the heat of him. His earthy scent that twisted her insides into complicated knots. He murmured in her ear, 'I may be the Dastardly Duke, but I do believe in doing things properly. Even this.'

Lance released her and she wavered. She sucked in a deep breath, trying to remind herself this was all fake. Men like him didn't fall for women like her. Then he took both of her hands in his, his warm, solid grip holding her steady. He stared deep into her eyes and she lost herself in the fathomless green of his, the golden fleck in them that gleamed like the opal in his pocket. So serious, so sincere. She had trouble breathing, getting any air.

'Sara.' His voice hit her like a shot of schnapps, sliding through her veins, straight to her heart. He was intoxicating. A girl could get quite drunk on him.

'I'm no prince. In fact, you'll come to learn I'm more toad than frog so, luckily for you, none of this is real. However, I'll do my level best to duel any dragons that come to your door in our brief time together...' He smiled down at her and everything ignited. 'If you think that'll do. That it's good enough for a woman who was once destined to be a queen. Will you do me the immeasurable honour of becoming my fake fiancée?'

She swallowed the lump forming in her throat and looked down at the ancient cobblestones in this dim back lane, somehow separate from the bustle of London, in a world of their own, and blinked away burgeoning tears. His proposal, for this crazy arrangement, was more romantic than her own real one had been. When she'd become engaged to Ferdinand, he'd simply pronounced, *'It's time we made this official.'*

'Of course,' she said to the stones underfoot.

'I didn't hear you. Don't tell me you're having second thoughts about the sincerity of my false declaration. A man's ego might not stand it.'

She bit her lip to stifle a giggle. Trust Lance to make her laugh. Sara chanced a look at him and he smiled, wide and bright. It was enough to warm her on this chilly day.

He raised an eyebrow, tapping his foot in mock impatience. 'I'm waiting.'

'Yes. I'd love to be your temporary fiancée.'

'Excellent.' He took her hand and slid the ring onto her finger. It was warm from his touch and fitted perfectly. Sara didn't believe in signs, so why did this feel like a portent of…something? She placed her hand to his chest, the strong muscle firm and hot underneath her palm.

'Thank you. For saving me.'

A look passed across his face. Not a shadow, exactly, but something dark and thrilling nonetheless. Then it was replaced by a flash of heat and, even though she wasn't experienced in many things, she recognised that look. The flare of his nostrils as he cupped his hands either side of her jaw. All of this made it impossible to think, witnessing the…intent written over his face. Her lips parted to sip at the air because a tight band had wrapped round her chest and squeezed. His eyes flicked to her mouth, caught there.

'Lance?' Her voice was husky and low, sounding nothing like her at all.

'Let's take a moment to savour this unique event.' His thumbs brushed her cheeks and a tremor ran through her which had nothing to do with the cold breeze blowing down the lane. Then he dropped his head. She knew what was coming and, even though this was fake, she felt a heady rush of anticipation. Sara closed her eyes as his warm breath brushed across her skin, leaving tingles in its wake. Lance was so close the heat emanated from him as he held himself a sliver away. He was waiting for her, she knew, to say no if this wasn't what she wanted. But oh, how she *craved* him.

'*Sara.*'

The whisper of her name brushed her skin and she was lost to him, closing the minute distance between them to press her lips to his, her kindling to his spark, and she ignited. His mouth moved over hers, gentle and coaxing. She sighed into him as his arms slid round her and drew her

close, melting as his tongue dipped, touching hers. A question which she answered by opening for him, slipping her arms round his neck and drawing him down. He plundered then, invaded her, and she gasped at the slick seduction of it all, tasting and teasing each other in a lonely lane in the middle of London, where the world rushed round them and could end for all she cared. This glorious moment witnessed only by the old stones.

Sara was lost in it but Lance slowed, his mouth luxuriating over hers before easing to a stop as he drew away. He glanced up the lane briefly, eyes narrowing, then turned back to her, removing his hands from her cheeks. She felt the loss of him to her very core. Her heart pounded against her ribs and everything tilted on its axis. Did it tilt for him too? She couldn't really tell, though a slight crease had formed between his brows. Maybe she'd done it all wrong? She was scared she had and didn't know why it mattered.

Then he tucked a loose curl behind her ear. Traced the shell of it with his finger and his touch sparked across her. His lips tilted into something enigmatic.

'I hope that was better than *moist*.'

She rocked back on her heels. It was about that? A strange sense of ego? Because her past had no part in what was going on here. Ferdinand was a mere shadow against this vibrant, elemental man.

She began shivering and it had nothing to do with the chill breeze that swirled around them.

'Come on, you're cold. If we're done ring shopping—'

'Don't you have to pay?'

'John and I have an understanding. Let's say farewell and take you home.'

They walked back into the shop, hand in hand.

'Congratulations.' John rounded the counter with his arm outstretched, vigorously shaking Lance's hand. Then he leaned over and kissed Sara on the cheek. 'I never thought I'd see the day.'

'Me neither,' Lance said. 'But all it took was a special woman.'

He looked at her and smiled, and she wanted to believe in that. She really wanted to believe.

CHAPTER FIVE

SARA STRETCHED, BASKING in the cool early morning sunshine that flooded the glorious bedroom of the Duchess suite. It had been a whirlwind since arriving at Lance's magnificent home by helicopter the previous afternoon. She'd been introduced to the small yet enthusiastic staff. George, the butler, seemed especially determined to find out everything about the workings of Morenburg Palace and her own family's manor, her likes and dislikes, so she could feel at home here.

Then there had been a brief tour of the public areas of the house, before a personal shopper had arrived with an array of clothes that fitted the description of what she wanted *perfectly*. It boggled Sara's mind, given the limited time the woman had to pull it all together. It also told her a great deal about Lance's power and influence.

He'd arranged a quiet dinner for her in her room when she'd begun to fade from the stress of the past two days. He was more attentive as a fake fiancé than her real one had ever been. She'd never really felt like royalty, even when she had the chance of being royal. But the way she'd been treated in this house made her feel like a princess...

Dangerous, Sara.

She had to keep reminding herself. She knew where romantic delusions had led her once before and couldn't do that again. Believe in love. Be cast aside. She shrugged off those thoughts and peered at the doorway which led to a shared en suite bathroom and walk-in wardrobe separating the Duke and Duchess's suites. Lance had said it was a recent addition to the house, designed by his sister, who'd helped redecorate. But it wasn't the elegant interior design she was interested in. It was the fact that mere metres away Lance had slept…

She held up her left hand in a shaft of sunlight, watching the myriad colours glitter in her engagement ring, which she'd slipped on the moment she'd woken. She hadn't heard him overnight, collapsing into her lavish canopied bed and falling asleep the moment she'd hit the pillow. Her lips tingled and she brushed her fingers across them. Closed her eyes, imagining his coaxing mouth on hers once more. The way his arms slipped round her, holding her tight. It was okay. Her imagination couldn't hurt her, not here. But her body didn't seem to get the message, flushing hot, her heartbeat kicking up at the perfect memory…

Except.

She dropped her hand to her lap. Stood from the too comfortable couch in this beautiful room.

She'd been beguiled by dreams before. Powerful, handsome men made false promises. Lance at least seemed a little more honest than most, but she didn't want a permanent protector. Sara wanted to find herself, find her own way. It started today. She and Lance were going to a house an hour or so away. He'd been tasked with assessing the estate. Maybe she'd find something valuable and begin her quest for independence. That was the only thing that should excite her today.

Sara padded across the plush Axminster carpet to the walk-in wardrobe, not sure what to wear for today's expedition. She had mostly practical items, but there were a few lovely dresses she couldn't resist. Her clothes barely took up the allotted space, despite Lance's best efforts. She looked over at his side of the wardrobe. Rows of suits, shirts, ties and shoes, all perfectly curated. She shouldn't…but his domain tempted, through the doorway on the other side. She couldn't help herself…explore a little. What harm could it do? She still had plenty of time.

She brushed her fingers along the rack of exquisite suits hung in perfect order, the fabric soft and perfect. As she moved further into his space, she shut her eyes and breathed in deeply—something spicy and masculine, like cloves, but with a hint of sweetness. She snorted. As if anything about him was sweet. She effortlessly recalled the evil gleam in his eye and the wicked curl of his lip, sending delicious shivers right through her. She explored further, unable to help herself. In many ways he was a closed book, and this might give her an insight. The bespoke fine cotton shirts, hanging perfectly ironed with sharp creases. Silk ties in jewelled colours. She briefly wondered whether he ever wore causal clothes, until she found the worn jeans and soft T-shirts. She traced her hands over the fabric that had touched his skin, unable to help herself.

The door to his room lay *just there*. She peeked through but it was quiet. This was about the only regularly used room of the house she hadn't yet been shown. Her heart skipped at the illicit thrill of it all. But, for the sake of authenticity, shouldn't she, as his fiancée, have free access to his personal space? It made perfect sense, so she boldly walked on through.

If the Duchess suite was feminine, Lance's was undeniably masculine. There was a canopied antique cedar bed, with hangings that made it look as if a king slept there, still unmade. And she couldn't get out of her head that *he'd* slept here. The indentation on his pillow where his head had lain. The sheets, crumpled in disarray.

Had he dreamed about anything last night? Their kiss, perhaps? The warmth of that thought coursed through her. Did he sleep clothed? Naked?

That vision embedded in her brain like a splinter, because she'd seen enough of his body in the press photographs to know he'd be magnificent with nothing on at all. And that thought froze her to the spot. She should leave, but she couldn't make her feet move out of the room that embodied him so completely. All saturated, bold shades of greens and blues. Solid yet elegant furniture. Rich, soft fabrics. Decadent and sinful—a perfect reflection of the man himself.

As she stood, staring at the unmade bed where his body had lain, a voice called out from her room, coming closer.

'Sara?'

He walked through the doorway from the walk-in wardrobe on this side. She froze, not knowing what to do, because she was in his space but wore only what she'd slept in—a cute tank and sleep shorts in a silky soft fabric. Great for comfort, but not designed to hide much. His eyes widened as they met hers, then did a slow survey of her body. A lazy smile slid across his face. Her nipples tightened traitorously.

He'd be able to see everything. All she could do was brazen it out...

'I... I was just...'

'Exploring?' Lance leaned against the door jamb, preventing any kind of escape. His gaze flicked to the bed and back to her as the heat rushed to her cheeks. 'Do you like what you see so far?'

Sure, he was talking about the house, but all she could see was him. He wore dark, perfectly tailored suit trousers and one of those bespoke shirts, in a blue and white stripe. A gleam in his eye and a sensual curl of his lip spoke of all kinds of trouble. He was perfect. She couldn't take her eyes from him.

'It's a beautiful house.' She cleared her throat, and he raised an eyebrow. She tried to get the conversation on track. 'You must be very happy here.'

'We barely spent any time here as children, with my father's ambassadorial work. Sometimes it's nice to be back, but I spend most of my life in London. Is there anything more you'd like me to show you?'

'You must be wondering what I'm doing in here,' she said, sure she was the colour of the prize-winning beetroot the cook had talked of growing in the kitchen garden.

'You're the lady of the house now. For a little while at least. You're welcome to unfettered access.'

The thought of him, naked in bed, granting her unfettered access to his body, flashed through her consciousness. She heaved in a quick breath, heat blistering across her cheeks.

He pushed off the door jamb and came into

the room with her, then went to a velvet-covered armchair and picked up the navy-blue bathrobe draped across it. He held it out to her.

'This might make you feel less…exposed.'

She took the plush dark fabric and slipped the robe on. It was warm, soft, and smelled as delectable as him. He walked up to her and took the belt, tying it tightly round the waist, as if she were some child. The garment swamped her. How mortifying. Here she'd been fantasising about him naked in bed and he'd thought she was flaunting herself. She shuffled her feet, looking at the floor.

'Why don't we go into your room now? I have something to show you.' His voice was gentle. When he turned and walked back into the Duchess suite, she followed. She found him sitting on the floral chintz couch, overlooking a view of the rambling rose garden. Sara sat at the other end, but even that was too close.

He pulled his phone from his pocket, flicked to something on the screen and handed it to her.

'What's this?'

'An article in one of the tabloids.'

On the screen was a series of photographs of them in the lane yesterday. His hand to her cheek, looking into her eyes. Then the kiss. The way they looked at each other, simmering, intent. Lance slipping the ring onto her finger. That private moment, invaded. The headline shouted *'Debauched Duke Domesticated!'*

'How?'

He leaned back on the couch, hands behind his head, looking smug.

'There's usually significant interest in me but, on this occasion, I gave them a hot tip.'

She had a nasty feeling in the pit of her stomach, as if something had congealed. Silly. It was an excellent reminder that everything about this was fake. She'd thought maybe he'd been lost in the moment too. But no, it had only been her. Anyhow, what did it matter? Dashing dukes and handsome, aristocratic men weren't on her agenda. She straightened her shoulders and handed the phone back to him.

'So I'm guessing everyone knows now.' Why did her voice sound so quiet and hurt? She cleared her throat. 'Excellent.'

He frowned, then leaned towards her. 'You wanted a scandal, and you certainly have one now. Since it's public information, your parents will no doubt be aware. As will Annalise.'

She hadn't thought of that. When she'd checked her phone she'd ignored all the messages. She couldn't discuss this with Lise, not yet. And perhaps she didn't know yet, being on her honeymoon, hopefully immersed in wedded bliss…

'Thank you. Good job.' She smiled then, but it

felt fake to the core. That smile reserved for her parents, Ferdinand. The type of smile she'd promised herself she'd never give again…

'I'm pleased you're happy. Now, back to work.' He didn't look pleased, though. His frown remained. 'We'll be leaving in half an hour. You won't earn a commission if you don't find something worth selling.'

That was fine, excellent even. It was clear he wanted her out of his life. She wouldn't stay anywhere she wasn't wanted longer than absolutely necessary.

'I need to—'

'Put on some clothes… Of course. Take your time, and when you're done—' he stood and moved to the doorway, gave her a wink '—let's go and find some treasure.'

Lance held the steering wheel in a death grip. George had *not* been happy about him driving, had insisted that *Lady Sara* would expect a chauffeur. Good grief. His normally composed butler had finally cracked. Next the man would be breaking out the family Limoges dinner service and demanding they dine in the grand ballroom. It seemed to be all he could do not to wrestle the keys out of Lance's hand and drive them both to the next town for their fossicking expedition.

Lance hadn't really considered what it would be

like, bringing a supposed fiancée into the house. Especially not one so…qualified as Sara for the role of Duchess of Bedmore. She was perfect in every way. Lance took his eyes from the narrow country road and glanced at her, staring out of the window, captivated by the vibrant country-side around them. She was wearing some exquisite pale yellow floral perfection of a dress. She looked like sunshine, with what appeared to be a thousand tiny, distracting buttons up the front. He had an irrational desire to undo each one slowly…

No. As much as he tried to project an image of wickedness, he was *better* than this. It was seeing her this morning, that was all. In the past twenty-four hours he'd broken a few of his carefully crafted rules. There were many things he shouldn't have done. Acquiring an engagement ring which slipped onto Sara's finger so perfectly it was as if it was meant to be. Proposing with words that left her eyes gleaming with tears and tugged at his unfeeling heart, seeming all too real for his cynical soul. Kissing her soft lips, which had the hit of a drug and left him addicted and craving.

But the most stupid thing he'd done in this litany of foolishness was freezing like a dumbstruck teenager as she'd stood next to his bed, rather than turning and walking straight out of the room, leaving her be.

He hadn't wanted her to find those articles in the tabloids herself, or that was the excuse he'd told himself. That was why he'd gone to her room early. Then he'd found her and his downfall was complete. She was all glorious blushes and stuttering apologies when he'd been *thrilled* to find her in his space in sleepwear that clung to her beautiful body, looking at his unmade bed with a distant kind of longing that filled him with a surge of heat.

He hadn't been able to help himself. His gaze devouring her long, pale limbs...the golden curls tumbling round her shoulders...the tight nipples pressing against the fabric of her top. He shifted in his seat, the car becoming uncomfortably warm. What he wouldn't have given to sink into the covers, mussed from a sleepless night, and bury himself in her until they both forgot their names...

Which was generally the expectation when a woman was in his room, under ordinary circumstances. But not Sara. He might have spent most of his adult life cultivating a certain reputation but there was no requirement to uphold it, not with her. His job was to protect the woman, not debauch her. As much as he'd failed in the past, he'd make sure he didn't here.

Because as soon as that news story had hit, he'd received a stream of furious messages on his phone. Sara's family, making all kinds of accusations, demands and threats. The accusations he relished, especially from her brother, with whom he had a close to hostile history from school. He took a hand from the steering wheel and rubbed the side of his neck where his scar prickled as a reminder. As for the demands, he ignored—

'Are you all right?' Sara asked, taking her eyes from the road.

'Of course,' he said. Yet a flicker like a pilot light lit inside his chest. That she should care about him, when she was the one in need of protection. Her family's threats… He'd be damned if she was going back to that cold little alpine country where she'd be married off to some dolt who wouldn't care for her. *He'd* care for her, make sure no harm befell her. Protecting her was a chance to begin atoning for his multitude of sins.

They arrived at the stately, if somewhat worn-looking, house. Weeds invaded the gravel drive where they pulled up outside. He did the polite thing and opened the door for her, and then they were let into a dim front entrance by a member of staff. Lance's professional eye immediately began assessing the property. Thinning rugs on the floor. Dust motes glittering in a single beam of sunshine. The place was cold because the heating hadn't been turned on. The house spoke of gradual disrepair.

He'd seen it many times before. Families prioritising keeping up with their peers, forgetting the upkeep required for a property such as this. Then death arrived, with poorly planned inheritance and taxes, which was where he came in. His heartbeat picked up and he flexed his fingers. It always hit him the same way the minute he walked into one of these places. The excitement of the unknown, the quest to find incredible treasures hidden away for centuries.

He hoped it would excite Sara too, bring her out of the inertia that seemed to cloak her in this moment. Her smile was tight, the joy in it somehow subdued. She was probably bothered by the way he'd stared at her earlier like a leering teenager. In truth, he still couldn't keep his eyes from her. The gentle sway as she walked allowed the beautiful dress to twirl about her legs. A bright cardigan was wrapped around her shoulders, embroidered with flowers, her legs encased in boots. She was every country fantasy brought to life. And right now she stood in this drab entrance hall, in the only shaft of sunlight filtering through the smudged windows, brightening up the space with yellow and flowers and her indisputable *glow*. Looking like some glorious spring garden, with her blonde hair a wild and wonderful tangle down her back.

'We'll start in the attic. I'll send my people to assess the rest of the items later.'

The open, lived-in spaces where the obvious treasures would be displayed. His staff could value those, see if there was anything that might be interesting for sale. His speciality had always been the hidden areas—cupboards, cellars, attics—where people hid their treasures as well as their secrets.

'Why here first?' It was the first thing Sara had said in a while, her voice soft and musical, stroking over his skin like a feather.

They were led up a set of stairs that creaked underfoot, and then through several doors that did much the same, as if they hadn't been opened for years. Then they were alone with a large key in a dim, confined space under the roof. There was a dry, aged smell of dust, but it wasn't in as parlous a state as many attics he'd come across. Disappointing—the more dust the better. This looked a little too tidy. He flicked on the light to enhance the natural sun coming through the skylight.

'This is where secrets are kept.'

Sara lifted a dust cover from some bulky piece of furniture and peered underneath. 'You like that, don't you? Finding things out about people.'

'There are too many secrets kept in this world. People who pretend to be paragons of virtue. I like uncovering them, even if it's only to satisfy my own curiosity.'

If he'd done any kind of job uncovering the sins

of Vic's husband, she might never have married. She'd have been safe.

'Treasure…secrets… You found a Caravaggio, but what secrets have you uncovered?'

He shrugged. 'Lost loves, grand affairs, erotic collections. You name it, I uncover it.'

'That's almost…voyeuristic.'

'There can be something quite salacious about it that piques my interest.'

He winked and she began to giggle. It was such a bright and beautiful sound. She'd had enough misery. This woman should be smiling for ever.

'You're incorrigible.'

Lance bowed. 'Yes. I'm irredeemable. No matter what will be said about your capacity to reform me.'

'I don't want to reform you, whatever that means. A scoundrel is what I asked for, after all.'

'You might amend your view if you saw the worst of me.'

She leaned up against a mahogany sideboard, cocked her head to the side. 'I'm not really sure I would.'

The moment lingered. It was as if she were trying to reach inside him and weigh his soul. Part of him wondered what she found. Another part dreaded her conclusion. Yet whilst she stood as if trying to judge his worth, all he could see was her next to his bed, looking at the space he'd slept in as if she were imagining him still there.

He broke the silence first, looking around the space. 'Sadly, this attic is too clean to find much. Give me something dirtier. That's where the greatest treasure is found.'

She let out a sigh, hands on her hips as she looked around. The moment passed, and he regretted ending it rather than seeing where it led. 'Where to start?'

'I'll take this end.' He pointed to one side of the room. 'You take the other and we'll meet in the middle. Take notes and photographs, then we'll swap sides and see if we've missed anything.'

They worked in silence. The dust covers hid ordinary things. Broken objects. Nothing of real interest. He glanced over at her. She was clicking a photograph of a painting propped against the wall, arching her back like a glorious cat, blowing an errant curl from her face and tucking it behind her ear. He grinned as she looked over at him, her blue eyes cool and calm.

'You said your father hated you doing this. What about your mother?'

'My mother? The dowager?' He laughed. 'She doesn't much care what I do.'

She had her schemes, of course. Like marrying him off to continue the inglorious Astill name, to do his duty like some stud bull. That would never happen.

'Will I meet her?'

'No. Come autumn she takes to the villa in Spain and winters there with some of her friends. By the time she comes back, no doubt you'll be settled elsewhere and sick of me. I'll be a distant memory.'

A pretty pink colour flushed across her skin. Maybe not so distant a memory, then. He liked that. He liked it too much.

'And what about your sister?'

'Perhaps at the upcoming charity polo match. She occasionally attends.' Except of late she'd missed so much. He suspected her husband refused to allow her to be seen in public unless she was accompanying him. Sometimes she called, made excuses, her voice tired, distant. A little slurred...

'She has such a talent for design and decorating. Astill Hall's interior is beautiful.'

It was one of the few things Vic's husband had allowed her to do. A job where he thought she wouldn't embarrass herself, something to occupy her so he could pursue his career and other...interests. But Lance hadn't cared, so long as it kept the man away from his sister.

'Victoria has a flair for two things. Interior design and saving abandoned creatures.'

Her husband didn't admire either talent.

'Your sister sounds interesting. I think I'd like her.'

Once, perhaps. Now... Vic's hidden talent was hurting herself, and those who tried to love her. He didn't understand how Sara could remain so seemingly untainted by all the ugly behaviour she'd been subjected to. How could someone still contain all the wonder and hope she appeared to have? Her fiancé, a philanderer and then dead before the wedding. Her parents, still trying to sell her off to the highest bidder to maintain the power and position they felt slipping through their bony fingers.

'Well, I'm done on my side.' She huffed out a breath, blowing a stray curl from her face. 'There wasn't much here. Except...'

The way those words drifted off, making him wait. Making him ask. He smiled. She was playing him at his own game. 'What have you found?'

'All I have is this.' She wandered over to a chest of drawers and rubbed her nose, pulling up an old shoe box. Inside was the flotsam and jetsam of a child's collection—old doll's house furniture, smooth river pebbles and figurines which Sara picked through.

'These—a collection of farm animals.' She lined them up on the top of a chest. They were hardstone, with glittering gem-like eyes. Then she looked up at him again with all that hope.

His heart stuttered with excitement because she
knew what she'd found and so did he, as much as
he could tell from the cursory glance.

'What do you think they are?' she asked.

He smiled. 'You *know* what they are.'

'Fabergé?'

He lifted one; it was cool in his hand. Still in
good condition, considering children had played
with them. Beautiful. Collectible. Valuable. 'I
think you might be right. Congratulations, Lady
Sara. If the family's keen to sell, these will be
your first commission.'

She stood in front of him, her lips parted, glorious curls framing her face. Looking at him as
if he held the answer to every question she'd ever
care to ask. She made him feel like King of the
world with that expression. Right then, he craved
to be the answer to all things for her. In an alter-
native universe where whatever she wanted and
needed he alone would provide.

When had he ever felt this way? Perhaps never.
He cherished every moment of the gift she gave
him—the belief he could offer something of value.
She reached up and pushed some strands of hair
from her cheek. A smear of dust was left behind
by her fingers.

'You have a mark.' He pointed. Sara rubbed
in the general area but missed the smudge mar-
ring her face.

'Let me,' he murmured. Lance smoothed his thumb over the spot. Her skin was silky and warm under his fingers.

'All gone now,' he said, about to remove his hand, which had lingered too long. Except she leaned into his touch, her eyes drifting shut in a long, slow blink. He froze, cupping her cheek. They were close, the warmth of their bodies mingling, curling through him. He dropped his head as she seemed to move up onto her toes. It would be one kiss. Celebrating her find. Surely that wasn't too much?

He leaned down and held himself a breath away from her, his whole body tight. The smell of her was like spring in the dusty attic.

'Congratulations, Sara,' he whispered against her lips as she reached for him and their mouths collided, hers soft against his own, opening for him. He slid his arms round her back and drew her hard against his body, her tongue hot and slick against his own.

He groaned as she thrust her hands into his hair, raking her fingers through. The scrape of nails against his scalp. Their mouths and teeth clashing as everything spun out of control. She ground herself against him, no air separating their bodies. He was so damned hard he could barely think, the moment all gasps and questing fingers. There were buttons on her dress, but he fumbled them.

Instead, he grazed his palms against her nipples, which were tight and peaked under the fine fabric. His mouth captured her throaty moan, pure bliss to his ears.

They were caught in some kind of madness and the end of the world wouldn't stop him, the desperate noises she made urging him on.

He lifted her, planted her on a covered sideboard which, thank the Lord, was the perfect height. She hooked her booted legs round his thighs and dragged him closer, the heat of her against the hardness of him as she panted his name. She dropped her head back and he kissed the column of her throat.

'You *love* this.'

His lips traced from her pulse point to behind her ear, and she shivered when he kissed her there.

'Yesss…' Her elongated hiss drove him on. He slid his free hand up her skirt, teasing at the silken skin of her thighs, slipping his fingers between them till he found her, slick and wet through her underwear. He began to rub her through the damp fabric, stoking all her banked heat. Nothing was more important in this moment than her pleasure.

'There are people downstairs who could hear, but you don't care, do you? I *knew* you'd be like this. So responsive.'

He kept the steady, swirling motion of his fingers against the centre of her, winding her higher and higher. Caught in the maelstrom of Sara's quest for pleasure, her hips moving in time to his fingers.

'How desperate can I make you? What will you do for me?'

He surged against her and she whimpered, her eyes glassy and unfocused. Her cheeks were a delicate shade of pink, the same colour flushing her chest and climbing the column of her throat.

'I need. I need…' It was like a chant.

'I know what you need.'

He didn't give a damn if all of the staff in this house stood at the attic door and watched them. He'd stop for *nothing*. He pressed a little harder, teased her soaked core.

'I have you,' he growled in her ear. 'Come for me like the good girl you want to be.'

She stiffened. Stopped breathing. Arched her spine as he crashed his mouth against hers, capturing her gasping sobs. He kept stroking in a steady rhythm, through wave after wave that had her convulsing in his arms, until she shuddered a final time and fell against him, soft and limp, resting against his aching body. His panting breaths lifted threads of golden curls on her head.

What he wouldn't give to push her underwear aside, slide into her and take her, now.

But sanity inched back. He wasn't a teenager. He didn't have protection. Then a creeping disgust prickled through his veins because he would *not* take advantage of her.

As much as he knew he should move away, as much as he ached for her, he merely held her against him. He felt her relax, stroking her back. Resting his chin on her head and breathing her in. Relishing her long, deep sigh of satisfaction, a bright kernel of glowing warmth illuminating his irredeemable soul.

Sara nestled into Lance's hard chest as her panting breaths eased. One part of her brain screamed *What have you done?* But those thoughts were smothered by the warmth of a man's strong arms round her, of her blood, sweet and thick like treacle, sliding through her veins. Sated. Protected.

She'd never felt like this before. Certainly not with the man she'd been supposed to marry. She knew pleasure on her own, of course, but this had consumed her, burned her, and now she felt new and tender. Easy to bruise.

Lance didn't shift, he didn't move. He just held her, and in his arms she felt like something precious and beautiful. Like the Fabergé animals he'd carefully held and caressed with his fingers. Something of true personal value. Whilst Lance still hadn't let go, she loosened her legs a little. The centre of her was pressed against him and he was still hard. She wondered why he wasn't doing anything. He had an obvious need, the mere thought of which started a tempting pulse low and deep inside her again. As if what had happened had broken something in her and all she could do was want and want and want.

'Are you okay?' His voice was rough, so he cleared his throat.

Okay? Merely okay? The whole of her still soared somewhere in the clouds. And the prickle of uncertainty needled at her as she crashed back to earth.

You'll never have his heart.

Those words taunted her, encapsulating the certainty that she was not loved, was valueless other than for what she could provide as a wife. She didn't want any man's heart, not after the painful lessons of her past. But what if she'd misunderstood Lance's desire? No. She couldn't second-guess. He'd looked at her and touched and, whilst she'd been the one to initiate the kiss, he'd been close, waiting for it. And there was no doubt that his body wanted her...

But now all the syrupy lassitude had dissipated with this fear that somehow she'd done something wrong. She pulled back, not quite able to look him in the eye.

'I'm fine.' How gauche she sounded, when what he'd done had ripped her apart. She blinked back the fierce tears burning her eyes, her nose. He'd made her feel…perfect and wanted. Why couldn't she hold her head high and accept it? Because she was worth *something* as a person, no matter what Ferdinand and her family might have thought.

Lance tipped his finger under her chin and she was forced to look into the cool green of his eyes as they tracked over her face, his brow furrowed in concern. If he saw the gleam of tears he wouldn't just think she was a *good girl*, but a silly little girl. Men didn't like those, as her mother had always told her. What they wanted were serene, self-contained women. Well, she could be just that.

'We should get moving. There's a whole house to explore.' She wriggled herself loose of him but, strangely, he didn't appear to want to let her go, slow to remove his arm, his hand. She slid from the sideboard, trying to put herself back together. Straightening her clothes. Reflexively running her hand over her hair.

'We should perhaps wait a few moments. Till I'm more…respectable.'

She looked at him, trousers pulled far too tight across his groin, his arousal impressive—and impossible to miss. She winced.

'Oh, do you need a…a hand or anything?'

He snorted. 'Whilst I haven't had to deal with an inconvenient erection since my teenage years, I think I'll survive.' The blood rushed to her cheeks.

She turned and attempted to take a few pictures of the figurines she'd lined up earlier, but her hand wouldn't stop shaking.

'Sara.' He gently placed his hand over hers, steadying it. 'I'm sorry if you're uncomfortable. It won't happen again. We got carried away.'

She took a deep breath. Great, good. Except someone needed to tell her body, which was still tingling all over at his nearness. The whole of her still soft, ready and far too willing to leap at him and demand a repeat performance.

A man like Lance wouldn't want her—if he'd wanted her, he would have done more. And there she'd been rubbing against him as if she were some feline overcome by catnip. Like Ferdinand when they'd spent their disastrous night together, Lance's physical reaction hadn't been to her as such. Any man would react that way to a woman wrapping herself around him and clinging like some rampant creeper. Anyhow, she needed to stand on her own two feet, not fall for her beautiful rescuer. Doing that would be a one-way journey to more heartbreak.

'There's nothing to apologise for, and nothing more to discuss,' she said. She turned to face him because she was going to be an adult about this. Sophisticated. She forced herself to look up at him. His hair was dishevelled, mouth redder than usual from their kisses. He looked down at her with a world of concern shining in his eyes. 'I had a nice time.'

He grimaced. Then nodded. Her hand was steady now, so she turned her back on him and began taking random photographs to give herself some space.

Lance was right. It was simply the intoxicating mix of the excitement of the moment and unrestrained hormones that had led them here. The adrenaline of finding her first valuable antique couldn't be avoided. But her hormones? From now on they were being kept well and truly under lock and key.

They had to be.

CHAPTER SIX

ON THE DRIVE back to Astill Hall Lance kept up a steady narrative on what they'd found and how much the figurines she'd discovered might fetch at auction. Sara was caught between wanting to scream at him to stop because he seemed so unaffected by what had happened and weeping in thanks that they could pretend nothing had happened at all.

Her body didn't lie, though. No matter how mortified she still felt, it wanted him with a ferocity of desire she'd never experienced before. The ache inside, the heat between her thighs. The prickle of her nipples, now uncomfortable in her bra. As if she was ripe, ready to be picked. If he pulled the car over, dragged out a picnic blanket and wanted to have his way with her under a tree at the side of the road she feared she would agree with indecent enthusiasm.

Proving she wasn't a good girl at all, but *bad*, as he'd first pointed out at the funeral months ago. Even more horrifying, she kind of liked it.

As they turned into the stately driveway of Astill Hall she was relieved she'd at least survived without begging him for a repeat performance or, worse, for forgiveness. The problem was, she wasn't sure how she *should* behave, so she was trying steadfastly to just ignore the fact that she'd orgasmed with Lance's hand stroking between her legs, murmuring those wicked words, making the fire inside her burn hotter…

As Lance parked the car in the expansive garage, George arrived to meet them. He looked from Lance to Sara and back again. Was it obvious something had happened? Surely not, and yet she couldn't help feeling that guilt was written all over her face. The air between them became stiff and uncomfortable as the silence stretched.

'Your Grace.' He nodded to her. 'Lady Sara.'

Lance raised an eyebrow. 'Is this the way things are going to be?'

She wasn't sure what any of this meant. As far as she was concerned, Lance's butler seemed to be behaving entirely appropriately. He would have fitted in with any of the staff at the Morenburg Palace.

'It's only proper.'

'When has anything in Astill Hall been proper?'

George stood a little taller. Glared at Lance. 'You have a fiancée. There are standards to be upheld.'

'You well know I've never been one for *standards* of any kind.'

'Perhaps you can maintain them for a little longer since you have a deputation. From the village.'

Lance snorted. 'Really? I've never had a deputation before.' He looked over to her, a grin on his face. 'I suspect I'm not the person they want to see. They're interested in someone else entirely.'

'Which is why I'm letting you know, in case Lady Sara wishes to…have some time before joining you.'

'Excellent idea. We're both in need of a moment.'

'I'll let them know you'll be with them presently.'

George left and Lance turned to her, his expression serious. 'Do you need anything—bathroom, cold water, a stiff drink? An excuse to avoid the next half hour or so?'

It was time to show him how unaffected she could be. 'No, I'm happy to meet your deputation now. So long as I look presentable.'

They'd cleaned up in a guest bathroom at the manor house before leaving, but she wanted to make a good impression, although she wasn't entirely sure why.

'You could never look anything other than beautiful.'

All her good intentions dissolved with his words, like a flame to candle wax. She wanted to melt to the floor. He held out his hand to her. She dropped hers into it without thinking and the warmth of his palm engulfed her. There was something about him that felt so safe, even though in reality he was her greatest risk.

They walked through the house, hand in hand. It didn't feel cloying, but as natural as breathing. She enjoyed the way he gripped her as if he was intent on holding her, as if she was more than an afterthought and this wasn't just something he was doing for the sake of appearances.

Dangerous, Sara. Dangerous.

George was waiting for them inside. He opened the door to a parlour where a small group of people sat. The minute they entered the room, the deputation stood and moved forwards. When Lance smiled it didn't look false and cold, like all the times she'd seen Ferdinand smile at his subjects. Lance's smile warmed the whole room.

'Good morning, Mrs Snow. I hope your husband is improving?'

The woman nodded. 'He is, sir. Our profound thanks for your consideration.'

'Whatever I can do.' Lance's gaze was full of sympathy. 'The village wouldn't be the same without your family.'

The woman's cheeks flushed as Lance turned to the others. 'Mr Bramwell, I hope your daughter's still enjoying university...' He went through the names of the six or so people there, making comments about their lives as they beamed at him as if he were the saviour of all things. 'What brings me this honour?'

Another woman in the group stepped forwards, gaze darting towards Sara. She was older than the rest, with a kind face. *Mrs Hutchins.* 'The honour's ours. We've seen the papers. We never believe what they say about you, but…is it true?'

'Ah, perhaps you should believe some things,' Lance said with a devilish grin. Everyone turned to her, eyes wide. 'I'd like to introduce you to my fiancée, Lady Sara Conrad.'

There was a collective inhale from the little group. Exclamations. Smiles. Everyone crowding her with genuine happiness. It was so infectious she couldn't help but be carried along with it.

'Our heartiest congratulations,' another man said, coming to shake Lance's hand as everyone clamoured around them. It seemed so surreal. She wasn't sure she'd received as much attention and affection in Lauritania when she was destined to be *Queen.*

One of the women passed a basket to Lance. 'It's not much. A few of us put some things together. Small tokens of our congratulations for you and Lady Sara.'

Lance lifted the cover laid over the basket and pulled out a jar topped with checked fabric and tied with a red ribbon. 'Mrs Perkins, is this some of your prize-winning gooseberry jam? You know it's my favourite.'

'It has been since you were a wee boy.' The woman beamed at him. 'But I still won't tell your cook the secret ingredient.'

Lance laughed. 'And I'll continue to ask.'

Mrs Perkins chuckled in response as the chatter carried on around them. Lance seemed to know who had made or grown everything in the basket, from the large brown eggs to the cakes.

Mrs Hutchins came up to her. 'Welcome to our blessed little part of the world. We hope you'll be happy here.'

'Thank you. I've yet to see the village.' What more could she say? She felt like a fraud, lying as she was. How would these kind people react when things inevitably ended? Would they blame Lance, given his reputation? Seeing them with him now, the thought that they might seemed so…unfair.

'You will. Whilst he spends much of his time in London, His Grace still takes a keen interest. I assume you'll be at the charity polo match? He always puts on food and drink for the locals. It's a grand show. He's quite the thing on horseback,' the woman said, lowering her voice in a conspiratorial way.

Sara hadn't thought much about it till now, but she'd seen enough photos when doing her research on him to know that Mrs Hutchins was right. Lance looked fine on horseback. He was, in fact, *fine* in all respects. She lifted her hand to brush back a strand of unruly hair, trying to ignore the blush creeping up her throat.

'What a beautiful ring. You're not wearing the Astill Amethyst?'

Lance joined them, the warmth of his body both a temptation and a strange comfort as he stood close. The pleasure of that heat slid through her as she leaned into him.

'Sara doesn't like purple, so I'd never inflict the amethyst upon her. That would make me a bad fiancé.' A few of the women seemed to blush as Lance's eyes took on a devilish gleam. 'But she looks beautiful in opals. I'll have to drape her in them. She should wear nothing else.'

He winked, and the little group of villagers laughed.

'He was always such a cheeky boy,' Mrs Hutchins whispered with an indulgent smile. 'Could get away with anything, and often did. But always quick to seek forgiveness. Raided my vegetable patch one day as a lad. Found him sitting in the dirt eating tomatoes like they were peaches. There went my attempt at making chutney. But then that afternoon there was a beautiful bunch of roses on my back step. Plucked straight from the bush. Astill Hall had a magnificent rose garden in those days. It's a bit wild now.'

'I love roses,' Sara said.

'That garden should be resurrected. Maybe now you're here...' The woman looked at her hopefully. 'I hope I'm not speaking out of turn. But some of us never thought we'd see the day a woman would grace Astill Hall again. This place hasn't had a family for as many years as I can remember, and it needs one. *He* needs one.'

Sara swallowed, not enjoying the lie she was required to perpetuate. She hadn't really thought through the consequences of accepting his offer, and she suspected he hadn't either. 'Lance is... independent.'

'He's a good man. And we weren't sure. We don't believe much of what the papers write about him, but this...it was too much to hope for, and yet here you are.'

Sara thought she saw brightness like tears in the woman's eyes. Happy tears for sure. It was all such a surprise. He had disdained the role of Duke of Bedmore, yet here, amongst the people from the village, he was warm and kind and...loved.

'Would you all like tea?' he offered behind her.

Mrs Hutchins turned. 'No, we'll be getting along. You'll no doubt have things to do. A wedding to plan.'

The group nodded enthusiastically.

'I'm leaving all of the arrangements in the

hands of my capable fiancée, and she tells me there's no rush to the altar.'

The group seemed disappointed. They shuffled and moved out into the hall, leaving the house.

'They adore you,' she said as he closed the door behind them.

Lance turned, his look sharp. 'No. They don't.'

She waved her hand to the door. 'Then why that? There was no need to come here and bring handmade gifts. It took effort.'

He shrugged and said nothing, his jaw hard as if he were grinding his teeth. 'This has been my family's seat for centuries. It's misplaced loyalty, that's all. Don't have any delusions about me, Sara. I'm not a good man.'

'But—'

'They've reminded me there are a few last-minute arrangements which need to be made for the match, and I need to see to the horses. Can I leave you for the afternoon?'

He'd shut the conversation down, his whole demeanour a warning to tread no further. Anyhow, an afternoon away from each other would be beneficial, allow her to regain her equilibrium, because right now she felt like someone on a boat who hadn't yet found their sea legs.

'Of course,' she said. If he wanted to maintain the façade that he didn't care, when it was clear to her that he did, then that was up to him. She wasn't going to be around for long enough to have to worry about it anyhow. But she couldn't help wondering…

Why did he believe he was so difficult to love?

Lance lay awake. It was well past midnight and it seemed sleep would be elusive tonight. He should be exhausted. He'd spent the afternoon in the stables, working hard with the stable hands to muck out the stalls and clean the tack till it gleamed, not as uncommon an occurrence as some might imagine. He'd always found that hard physical work to the point of exhaustion kept the demons at bay, during the night-time at least. Especially when sleeplessness was a common issue for him in this house, with its oppressive reminders of his unwanted obligations and inexpiable failings.

It wasn't exactly his failings keeping him awake tonight, though. Through the dark cavern of the doorway to his walk-in wardrobe flickered a dim blue glow that suggested Sara might be awake and on her phone. So close, yet so far.

It seemed she wasn't sleeping either. He had a few ideas about what could fix that, for them both, and the less circumspect part of him took the thought and grabbed hold with interest. Those glorious breathy moans of hers, the exquisite flush across her cheeks, head thrown back in ecstasy… Lance couldn't stop thinking about how she'd reacted in his arms that morning. The passion, the pleasure. How responsive she was to his touch, his words. It lit something in him like a fever, leaving him tossing and turning, the crisp cotton sheets scratching rather than slipping over his skin.

Hell, maybe it was these damned boxer shorts he'd put on in case he had to rescue Sara in the middle of the night from…he wasn't sure what. It had seemed like the respectable thing to do with a woman in the room next door. What if a rat or mouse ran into her room, and she was afraid? In such a situation, a lack of clothing might mean she couldn't accept his offer of assistance. He almost laughed at how he'd become so decorous. Except the only rat in the house was him.

This was more than mere desire. It was a vicious craving that flayed him alive. Yet here he lay, gripping the sheets of his bed in his fists to stop himself from going to her, when it was clear she didn't even want to talk about what had happened today, much less engage in a repeat performance. He'd almost made her *cry*, despite her attempt to hide it. The gleam of tears in her eyes was not something he could ignore. He'd been trying to protect her, and now he wanted to debauch her. None of the things he'd done in his efforts to ruin his family's reputation had bothered him before. This? She'd come to him for help and he couldn't keep his grubby hands away from her.

As he rolled over he noticed movement at the door connecting the wardrobe to his room. It was hardly noticeable, the hint of a shadow.

'Sara?' he whispered. 'Is that you?'

'I… Yes. I wondered if you were awake.'

His heart pounded at the soft lilt of her voice. And the memory of her throaty moans left him hard and wanting. But he was stronger than this. He leaned over and clicked on his bedside lamp, wincing at the suddenness of the light.

She stood barely inside his room, swamped in a huge, furry pink robe that looked as if a horde of soft toys had been sacrificed for its creation. He should sack the stylist for bringing such a thing into his house. Usually, the clothes she provided were sheer and tantalising silk, but Sara wasn't a lover who would enjoy the fruits of a fleeting liaison. She was supposed to be his fiancée, and perhaps that was the difference. Now, she looked soft and small like a kitten. Vulnerable and precious. In need of protection.

'Can't sleep?'

She shook her head, looking first at her toes and then at him. Her eyes widened slightly as she took in his naked chest. He grabbed the sheets and quilt and pulled them up slightly higher, as they'd slipped low. She watched every move, her pale blue eyes tracking over him intently. Heat burst across his skin.

'What's wrong?'

'My family's been in touch with you?'

'Yes, they're not happy with me.'

'They're not happy with me either.'

The difference was, he didn't care, whereas Sara appeared to. She moved a little closer to the bed and all his attention homed in on her. Her smooth, curved calves and slender ankles. He wondered then what she was wearing under the robe. That cute little ensemble from this morning, or maybe nothing at all…?

Of *course* she wore something. She wanted solace, not ravishing. He wrestled his imagination under control. He had a duty here. Stray erotic thoughts were not to be involved.

'I expect they won't be, but they seem to think it's all my fault for leading you astray, so you're in the clear.'

She came to the side of the bed slowly. The mattress dipped as she perched on the edge, as if she wasn't sure she should be there. He was sure she shouldn't. Lance gripped the sheets, lest he reach out and touch her. Sara looked down at her fingers.

'I was about to be married, to be Queen, and they're treating me like I'm some runaway child. I could understand why they might want me home if they were really worried, but it's not about me. They don't care about my choices. I've told them…' she plucked at the quilt, looking anywhere bar at him '…but it doesn't matter. I'm not important to them. I wasn't important to Ferdinand either.'

Sara's eyes were wide and sad, gleaming in the lamplight with more unshed tears. 'I liked to dream. Aspired to be the best queen I possibly could be. To serve my country. I hoped I'd finally come to mean something to…' Her voice choked and cracked. 'It all seemed so worthy, but I really didn't matter. I could have been any young, marginally presentable, virginal aristocrat. I'm interchangeable. I was to him, to my family. Perhaps even to my country.'

'No.' He wouldn't take this; she was worth so much more. Another precious woman in her prime, being manipulated for the purposes of others. He knew that script, the ending so painfully familiar. That would not be the ending for her. He sat up, leaned forwards and took her hand, clasping it in his. It was so cool and small. Fragile, trembling like her voice.

'They're the fools, Sara. Ferdinand didn't deserve you. He sought to carry on like his parents, whose marriage was propped up by nothing other than the weight of the crown. You think the King didn't have mistresses? I can give you some of their names. And the Queen. She didn't sit in her chambers knitting whilst her husband was entertaining. Be assured of that.'

Sara's eyes widened and her mouth dropped open, shock evident on her face. Perhaps he shouldn't have shattered her illusions about the now deceased royal family, but he could not sit here and watch her blame herself.

'I might not have lived in Lauritania for years,' he said, 'but my father was one of the King's friends, and Rafe is my friend. Nothing much is secret from me where that family is concerned.'

'So it wasn't his fault; it was how he was raised?'

'Never. It was all his fault. He could have tried to get to know you. Anyone who did that would see what I see. You're a beautiful, passionate woman who hoped for romance, yet understood her duty to her country. What was not to love, or at the very least admire? You deserved that.'

She deserved it all.

She turned away, but not before a tear dripped onto her cheek. 'And what of Annalise? She's married to your best friend.'

He blew out a long breath and thought carefully about his answer, because the truth was important to him, painful as it might be. Kind lies might assuage, but they were lies nonetheless. 'Your Queen was required to marry because of the constitution. Rafe is an ambitious man, a good man, an even better friend, but ambitious and cynical nonetheless. He won't cheat, but I'm not sure the marriage was a love match.'

'So the King doesn't believe in love, but he'll be faithful to their misery. Sounds wonderful.' She huffed and her lips compressed into a thin line. 'Do you believe in love?'

His heart thumped some anxious beats. In his experience, love was nothing more than a negotiation of interests, and never for him. He couldn't be trusted to protect anyone, and when you loved someone it was your duty to protect them for ever. Lance couldn't bear that responsibility, or the pain when he inevitably failed. Victoria's marriage had seen an end to that. But Sara looked hopeful. Did she ask that question because she was looking for love here? His palm began to sweat. He let go of her hand.

'I'm more cynical than he is. But don't ever lose the belief in something more. It's out there, waiting for you.'

'Ferdinand didn't love me. I'm not sure even my family do.'

What could he say? It was probably the truth. She hunched over, looking as if she were shrinking into herself more each moment.

'If that's the case, then they're fools.'

'You're being kind.' Tears glittered in her eyes. He hated them. She deserved so much more. He wanted to lay her down on the bed and kiss them away, turn the sadness into cries of pleasure. Replace that permanent look of disappointment. Make her smile, because her smile lit up the dark.

'Kindness isn't something I've ever been accused of. Do you think it becomes me?'

She huffed, but there it was, the merest raise of the corner of her mouth. For one moment that almost-smile made him feel capable of being whoever she needed him to be. She lifted her eyes to his, the hint of a flush across her face. 'It does.'

A pulse beat deep inside him, a sultry sensation that thickened his blood and made him want in a way that shocked him. He flexed his hands on the covers of the bed. Then her smile faded; it guttered and died like a candle snuffed out in the breeze. As if any happiness was as ephemeral as morning mist.

'My brother was...*is* the favourite. My parents coveted the fact that I'd be Queen, but Heinrich...' She looked at him, her eyes red-rimmed. 'Did your parents have a favourite?'

Her brother was spoiled, entitled and unworthy. As for him? The past, that old wound, ached once more. More bruised than sharp now, it had been with him so many years. Victoria had suffered because of that favouritism.

He shrugged. 'Aristocracy. The male inherits

the title, the females are married off. That's the way it is.'

'It's unfair. Would it be too much to ask to be wanted, not for what I can do but simply because I'm me?'

Her voice cracked and against all better judgement he leaned over and hauled her into his arms, wrapping them tight round her. She melted in his embrace, snuggling into him. He felt the warm drip of tears on his shoulder as her face nestled into his neck.

It felt right, *perfect,* but impossible all the same. This was a test, his penance. The price he had to pay for his past failures. Having her in his arms, but not being able to *have* her in the way he desired. Keeping her safe until she found her way, found her feet and left him.

Why did the thought cause something feral to howl inside him?

'Let me torment your family for you.'

'Can you do that?' Her voice was clogged and thick with tears.

'I'm an expert.' He'd made his parents pay for their failings. It was the least he could do for her.

'If you're asking my permission, I'm giving it to you.' She laughed then, a real sound of pleasure, her breath tickling against his neck. He shut his eyes, relishing the sensation of holding her close, the warmth of her against his bare skin. Her left hand was splayed on his shoulder, the scent of her surrounding him, light, bright and floral. His body began hardening, a pulse of desire beating hard, memories of her lips and tongue and panting breaths as she came apart in his hands flooding his mind.

She'd sense his arousal and he didn't want her to feel he couldn't control himself. Lance angled his body and placed her gently down on the bed next to him. Laid out on the covers, her golden hair spilled across the dark sheets, glowing pale and ethereal under the low lights.

'You should go to bed. Dream about your family suffering for their sins.'

He had a choice. To do what was right or what he *craved*. The problem was, in his life he mixed with those who were like himself—hedonists who knew what they wanted and took it without thinking because everyone around them wanted the same thing. Yet he had a greater responsibility. No matter how much he might want and want and want, his job here wasn't to take from this woman. She stared at him, eyes tracing his face. Lying there, bundled in her soft and fluffy robe, she looked all too innocent.

How he wished he could be innocent again, like her, with the belief that he was in some way a good man. But he was who he was.

Then she licked her lips and the movement

punched at the heart of him. A blistering heat flooded his veins, encouraging the pleasure-seeking side of him to take Sara, make her moan. She raised her arms above her head and arched like a cat basking in the sunshine of his worshipful gaze. Almost an invitation to touch. What he wouldn't give to stroke her, make her purr again. Then her lips parted, her voice a breathy whisper.

'What if I want to stay?'

CHAPTER SEVEN

LANCE WAS TRANSFORMED when she said those
words. He froze, not moving at all, as if he were
made from ice. When he'd laid her on the bed next
to him she'd hoped for something—another searing kiss perhaps? At least something to make her
forget. Her family's censure hurt, cutting to the
deepest bone and sinew of her. It seemed that so
long as she sat down, shut up and did what she
was told, they might deign to love her. Heaven
help her, wanting something for herself.

But ending up in Lance's arms again? The heat of
his touch, his strength…it had coursed through her
like molten gold, blistering and precious. And after
denying herself time and time again throughout her
life, a voice in her head had whispered, *Why not?*

Today what she'd experienced had made her
forget *everything*. There had been no pain, no
expectation, and she wanted to experience those
magical moments of being with him again and
again. They were both adults, why couldn't they
do this? Yet he made no move to touch her again.

The sheet had slipped to hug his narrow hips,
the soft light of the bedside lamp highlighting the
shadow-play on his sculpted torso. A body she
wanted to trace with her fingertips until they both

lost themselves in the glory of the sensation. Still, Lance only stared down at her as if she were an aberration in his bed, not a regular kind of occurrence, as the tabloids would have her believe. His pupils were dark, expressionless. He could have been carved from marble the way he lay on his side, propped on one arm. And realisation dawned. He didn't want her. Not really. Just like Ferdinand. That was why he'd made no move, despite her invitation.

Sara grabbed the front of her robe, clutching the edges together. There was no point making a fool of herself twice in one day. 'Okay. Right. I see.' She'd leave. They'd never speak of this again. She'd go back to her room, curl in her bed and die of embarrassment. She made to sit up.

'Sara.' Lance reached out a hand to cup her cheek, his palm hot against her skin. She stopped, lay back down. A tiny muscle in his jaw pulsed. 'Be sure of what you're asking me.'

She swallowed. A few words and there'd be no turning back. 'I am.'

The corner of his mouth kicked up a fraction. 'I'm not talking about sleeping.'

'Neither am I.'

'Good.' The word was a whisper against her lips as his mouth drifted across hers in an impossibly gentle kiss. When he pulled away, she rose to meet him.

'Patience. We have all night, and I intend to make use of every second of it to make you scream my name. Loudly, and repeatedly.'

She trembled at the thought of a whole night in his bed, in his arms. Lance undid the tie on her robe, opened the soft fabric that had become too hot. What she wore underneath wasn't seductive, practical sleep shorts and a top, because all the sheer nightwear she'd been presented with didn't seem like something you'd actually sleep in, more like something to model and then discard. She hadn't seen the point to it then, but she did now.

Except he looked at her with unalloyed hunger, reaching out a fingertip to circle a nipple pressing hard and aching against the soft fabric of her top. She closed her eyes and arched back into the bright burn of his hand, her breath coming in short, sharp pants.

'So responsive,' he murmured. 'A gift for me to unwrap.'

He slipped his hand under the shoulder of her robe and peeled it from her body, stroking down her back, easing into her shorts and cupping her backside, pulling her flush against him. Her hands roamed against the hardness of his chest, the dusting of hair prickling against her fingertips. He pinched her nipple with his free hand and rolled it between his fingers. She gasped, arching into him.

'You like that. What else might you enjoy for me?'

He did it again and she moaned, heat flooding between her thighs. His lips descended, teasing hers. She parted for him, and their tongues touched as she melted into the rhythm of the kiss. Not hard and taking, but something far hotter, gentle and coaxing, as if he was leading her slowly to anticipate the pleasure he'd promised. The care he showed cracked something inside her, emotion welling through her like lava from a volcanic fissure. He began to pull away and she chased the kiss, not wanting him to see how he was shattering her.

He didn't let her win that little battle between them. Lance rolled on top of her, the sheet and coverlet caught between them. The hardness of him pressed at the centre of her.

'You said you weren't exactly a virgin. What does that mean? It tends to be a state of being you either are or you aren't.'

His voice was kind but the words... They brought that horrible, humiliating memory rushing back. The searing pain. The disappointment. She shut her eyes, but it didn't stop her recollecting that awful night.

'Sara, we need to communicate. Whatever happened to you, it wasn't good, and I need to know because tonight's *all* about you.'

His thumbs brushed her temples, back and forth, soothing her. She had to get past this, the feeling that she somehow *lacked*, because of the way Ferdinand had made her feel that night. She took a deep breath and simply started.

'He said if we tried it might make our wedding night less fraught.' She wouldn't look Lance in the eye but stared at the ceiling over his shoulder, the ornate cornices embossed with gold leaf. His hands eased into her hair, stroking her scalp in a soothing rhythm. 'It sounded like a sensible idea. So we did. It…hurt a lot.'

The fingers in her hair clenched, and her scalp stung for a fleeting moment before Lance relaxed them.

'Tell me he stopped.'

His words were a hiss through clenched teeth. It had been her former fiancé's one act of kindness that evening. He'd stopped immediately. No attempt to comfort her, just a suggestion that things might be better if she had a few drinks beforehand, maybe at the wedding, then left her. Probably to go to his lover. How she'd tormented herself with that thought over the subsequent days, that her failure in bed had chased him away.

'Yes. He didn't…finish. He went away.'

Lance dropped his forehead to hers. 'Thank you for telling me. I know it was difficult.' His voice was soft, soothing. 'But in this bed I want you only to have pleasure, and to do that I need you to feel able to tell me what you don't want, as much as what you do.'

'What if I'm not really sure what I want?'

The corners of Lance's lips curled in a smile of unadulterated wickedness. His hips flexed into her and the feel of him, hard between her legs, almost made her eyes roll back into her head. As she moved to meet his rhythm, a tantalising pressure began to build deep inside.

'Trust me when I say I have plenty of ideas of what it will take to have you an unintelligible mess of sensation in under ten minutes.'

Her breath caught. There wasn't enough air in the room. Her head spun because the *intent* in his words…

'You sound very certain of yourself.'

He grazed his teeth over the shell of her ear, his breath teasing her throat.

'I am,' he growled. She slid her hands beneath the waistband of his boxer shorts, grabbing the taut muscles of his backside, her nails digging hard into his flesh and trying to pull him closer as he continued to rock against her body.

'Too many clothes,' she panted into his mouth and felt his smile against her lips.

'Greedy. We're doing slow.'

The explosion of that promise roared through her as she shivered with need. He pulled away, and she might have whimpered as he closed his mouth over the fabric of her top and sucked at her nipple, raking his teeth over the tight bud then sucking some more, the sensation arrowing like an electric shock between the juncture of her thighs. He turned his attention to her other nipple, which wasn't quite as sensitive.

'You prefer the left to the right. I'll remember that.' He lifted her top high, settled on the left nipple once more, sucking, teasing with his teeth. Slipping his hand down below the waistband of her sleep shorts, but not to where she wanted him most, teasing but never going far enough. Driving her wild until she twisted and squirmed underneath him, trying to get close, to rub her aching core against him. Then he stopped. She let out a moan of frustration and he chuckled.

'I reward good girls who do what I ask.' Heat flashed over her. If self-combustion was possible, this bed would be her funeral pyre. 'Lie still.'

She obeyed immediately. His smile was pure wickedness as he leaned over her, kissing down her chest, her belly, settling himself between her thighs. He grabbed the waistband of her shorts and she felt his breath at the centre of her as he slid them from her body.

'Open your legs wider,' he murmured, his lips teasing as he skimmed his tongue over her inner thighs. Her legs relaxed as she panted his name over and over. 'That's it. So perfect for me.' He settled between them, easing them wider till she was splayed out like an offering on the altar of his bed.

'I can't wait to taste you. It's all I've dreamed of.'

He'd dreamed of this?

'Please...' she moaned, not caring how wanton it sounded, the burning ache raging between her thighs making her lose her mind, all of her one bright, burning nerve-ending. He didn't move, just looked at her, thumbs circling close, but never close enough, his breath between her legs, warm on her oversensitive flesh. Her thighs trembled in anticipation.

'So sweet and wet for me.' His tongue licked the centre of her and she arched her back, bright lights bursting behind her eyes. There was no time for her to think about what he was doing, or that she should perhaps be embarrassed, with his tongue at the heart of her, his mouth working a slow rhythm. Licking, swirling, sucking. She closed her eyes because she couldn't stand it any more.

He stopped. 'For now, lie back and enjoy. Soon enough I'll have you watching me pleasure you.'

Lance centred on her clitoris. Nothing carried any meaning bar the burst of delicious agony between her thighs, his tongue concentrating on one tiny spot where her world entirely focused. Circling and driving her mad. She thrust her hand into his hair, gripping tight and holding him in place, as if it would end her if he moved away. The harder she held, the slower he went until all she felt was the impossible light flicking of him, and she writhed against his mouth, trying to get closer, saying unintelligible things, begging for release from the agony of it all. He didn't relent, the sensual torture seemingly endless. As if she were the most delicious dish imaginable and he was savouring her. Each time she came close he eased off, and she hated and adored him in equal measure as she trembled in ecstasy.

Then she felt it, at the entrance of her. A finger, pressing and easing inside. Sliding out and moving in again in a relentless rhythm, until it was joined by another. She moved her hips in time with his ministrations, the circling of his tongue, the thrust of his fingers. Then he curled them, touching a place deep inside. Her hips lifted from the bed and his mouth sucked hard at the heart of her. She wailed as the white-hot scorch of an orgasm tore through her body, wave after wave of agonising spasms wrecking her completely.

He brought her down gently, kissing her inner thighs, stroking her as she sobbed, tears streaming down her cheeks and she didn't care.

Losing her mind had never felt so good.

Lance took a glorious moment to absorb the beauty of Sara Conrad, gasping and unintelligible, sobbing with pleasure. Sleep shirt rucked up. Legs splayed wide. He gloried in the sensation, his name on her lips a benediction. Spread out on the sheets of his bed like a wicked offering. Utterly wrecked. He moved up her body, stroking, soothing, as he anticipated the next moments, of *finally* being inside her, hot and perfect.

She moaned at his touch and he allowed her to catch her breath, to glory in the sensation of her first orgasm at the hands of another. Then he kissed her luscious cherry lips and she almost devoured him, arching her body into his palms. He needed fewer clothes, nothing between them, close to being swept away by the wave of passion between them. He wrestled off his boxer shorts, the last vestige of his attempt at respectability stripped away, and carefully slipped Sara's top from her limp, replete body so she lay, flushed and glorious, on the bed before him.

He craved to rush, pound into that glorious soft body of hers till she screamed his name again. But she deserved his time, his selflessness. His hands trembled as he sought out protection and sheathed himself. How long had it been since he'd been like this, almost out of his mind with desire? Like a teenager all over again, when life still seemed full of possibility and promise. All he wanted was to be inside the warm dark heart of her and lose himself, carry them away from the reality of how temporary this was.

He crawled over her. Dropped his mouth to her favoured left nipple and used his teeth and tongue until she was writhing and begging once more, pleading to be sated. He was so damned hard he was terrified he wouldn't last, wanting her mindless again before he entered her, so he could keep his promise that this bed was about pleasure. He slid his hand between her legs, delving inside as she rocked into his palm, so wet and swollen with arousal it almost undid him. Then he positioned himself over her, notched at the centre of her body, and began sliding home, easing inside her until she was praying and moaning his name over and over. He stilled as she gasped. Held, seated deep inside her until she became used to him, kissing her slow, lush and deep.

'Let me show you how I *own* you.'

He moved. Slowly at first, gently rocking, till her legs wrapped round his waist and her heels jammed into his back, driving him hard. He took her with firm thrusts, buried his head in her neck and breathed in the heady scent of flowers and hot, aroused woman. Harder and harder, glorying in the digging of her nails in his back, the slick slide of bodies coming together.

Starbursts behind his eyes told him he was close. The way she clenched round him warned him she was too. He gritted his teeth against the prickle at the base of his spine, wanting her to come first, panting through the impending ecstasy as she ground against him, moaning, *'Please... please...please...'*

He lifted on his arms, looking down on her, head thrown back, eyes heavy-lidded and vacant with ecstasy, taken to some other place he'd soon follow as he thrust, keeping up a relentless rhythm. He dropped his gaze to where they were joined, the eroticism of that sight almost undoing him.

But her first. Always her.

'Angel. Look at *us...*look at what I'm doing to you.'

The words were a command and he loved how she obeyed, coming out of her reverie, lifting her head from the pillows to watch between them, her eyes glassy, almost unfocused.

He changed his angle. A tilt and twist and it ended her. She arched, falling back, screaming to the room and convulsing around him. The sensation ripped up his spine, rending him in two. His mind blanked with white-hot ecstasy, her name on his lips like a prayer of thanks.

Lance dropped to her, their bodies slick, pressing feather-light kisses over her neck as she came back to herself moment by moment. Her warm, gentle hands slid over his back as they remained joined. He'd move in a moment, but this… In his long and privileged experience, he'd never enjoyed anything like it. It rocked him, and in a recess of his barely functional brain he knew it was… *more*. This woman in his arms, in his bed, was *everything*. He could barely catch his breath. He wanted her again and again. He was still hard inside her. He could take her now, wanted to. He felt insatiable. It should have terrified him, but all that settled over him was a gloating kind of contentment.

Sara untangled her legs from around his back with a sigh as he slid out of her. Coherence was still piecing itself together, sensible thought blown apart. Somewhere in the fog of lingering pleasure he knew this should be worrying him, but as his body hummed, replete, he really couldn't care.

'Is it always like this?' she whispered, her voice hoarse. A pulse of ego thumped through him, that he'd done this to her.

Never…

But he couldn't admit that, or the truth of what they'd both experienced.

'Yes…if you know what you're doing.'

The lie wrapped its sharp tendrils round him, digging in hard, because he was not doing justice to what they'd shared. But there was no point romanticising this for her, or waxing poetic about what had happened in this bed. This was short-term, not for ever. Even though every nerve in his body screamed in violent disagreement that short-term wouldn't be long enough to sate him. Medium-term, he bargained. He'd tire of this before then.

He had to. He couldn't keep her.

A smile curled on Sara's pink, well kissed lips, and an egotistical pleasure curled through him. 'Then you must *really* know.'

'I like to think so.'

He rolled away from her and his confusing thoughts, leaving the bed to deal with the condom. Splashed cold water on his face to bring him back to his senses. Recently, even though he was only thirty-two, he'd felt old. Knew without a doubt he was jaded. But when Rafe had married... somehow imagining his best friend and partner in crime being...*domesticated* made settling down seem almost tempting.

He shook his head. It was a marriage of necessity for the Lauritanian Queen, and one of ambition for Rafe. Still, Lance had assumed that he and his friend would be the last bastions of bachelorhood. But tonight, with Sara in his arms, something else roared through him. As if he were eighteen again, with his whole life ahead of him. It was intoxicating, that sense of possibility, the same as when he walked into an old house full of hidden treasures. He didn't know what to do with that. And it didn't bear thinking about, so he returned to the bed where Sara lay.

She looked at him and stretched, but in her eyes he could see a small shadow of uncertainty. There was no way that could remain. In this bed, Sara shouldn't feel uncertain about anything. He stalked towards her, beautiful and wrecked, her skin flushed pink with grazes here and there from his growing stubble. Marks he'd made. A rush of blood coursed through him. Her eyes dropped to his groin and it was his turn to smile. There were advantages to everything feeling so new and fresh. He was hard for her again and from the way her eyes fixed on him with hunger it was clear she wanted him too.

'I hope you're ready to get no sleep tonight.'

Her eyes widened, and then her lips curled into a seductive smile. He hadn't wanted to touch her, but it was done now. He'd have time for regrets later, when this was over. By then, he hoped to have obliterated all unpleasant memories from her head for ever.

'Weren't we supposed to be doing something tomorrow?'

'Yes.' He'd planned a stroll through the village, but that could wait. He wanted as many of these glorious moments, losing himself in her, as he could get. 'We're spending the day in bed.'

CHAPTER EIGHT

POLO PONIES THUNDERED ACROSS the field. Bodies clashed. Sara flinched. Lance was in the thick it all, chasing a white ball on the ground somewhere. Her heart thrashed in her chest, part thrill, part terror. He had given her a quick lesson on the rules before they'd left for the charity polo match, organised to raise money for women escaping domestic violence. He said she needed to know when to cheer for him. But she didn't want to cheer. It looked dangerous, with large and seemingly uncontrollable horses racing around, jostling each other. Riders with mallets held high.

A pony broke free of the rough and tumble. *Lance.* Whilst she didn't know much about riding, she knew instinctively the man was an expert. He looked as if he were part of the horse, strong thighs gripping the saddle. She might have had heated fantasises about him, seeing the pictures of him on horseback when she'd searched him online, but looking at the man for real, face intent, directing some huge animal seemingly with the power of thought alone...

The heat of it speared through her and her breathing quickened. He was a magnificent animal himself, all taut, controlled muscle. She ached to have him alone somewhere, anywhere. Who knew she could have become so...wanton? No pretence any more. Working side by side during the day, with the excitement of finding treasure, and their nights entwined with each other. Heat pooled, deep and low, in her abdomen, all of her soft and willing and ready. Those memories. Making love till exhaustion claimed them, snatching sleep, making love again.

No. Not making love. There was no love here, was there. This, them, was only temporary. She'd never really been loved, she recognised. Not by her parents, or Ferdinand. She wondered what it was about her that was so...undeserving. The cut of that thought sliced deep. A sharp pain that could almost cleave her in two. This sensation with Lance *wasn't* love. It was something else. Dark, sultry. Moments of headiness that made her giddy. Though why did the merest thought of it being over make her want to curl in bed for days and weep?

The crowd cheered; they were quite uproarious given the supposed refinement of its members. Though champagne was flowing freely, which probably added to the rowdiness of the group. She took a sip of said champagne, then cheered along with them. Men. Women who stared out at the field. Stared at her, some with curiosity, some with daggers unsheathed. Though most interest was reserved for Lance. He was like the centre of the solar system for everyone there.

The match ended, and it seemed Lance's team had won. He leapt from his current mount, a magnificent chestnut now gleaming with sweat, pulled his shirt out from his polo whites and wiped his face, showing a slice of toned, muscled abdomen she knew came from hard exercise, but also hard work, particularly in the stables.

She shivered, the anticipation of a celebration tonight coursing through her. She wondered whether, in the rough and tumble of it all, he'd have any injuries. She'd kiss them better. She'd kiss him all over. Lance had been a passionate, attentive lover who was not shy about telling her explicitly what he enjoyed. An announcer droned in the background as the crowd returned to other things, drinking, eating. She couldn't wait for the afternoon to end. Because tonight…

'You're a surprise.'

The clipped haughty tone of a woman's voice pulled Sara from her heated fantasies. She turned. A woman with a champagne glass held casually like an afterthought in long, manicured fingers. Everything about her was tailored and perfect. The gleaming golden hair casually curled at the ends, no unruly tangles there. Blue eyes, darker than her own, leaning to grey, were cutting and cold. The smile on her face was sharp like a blade, make-up expertly applied to look barely-there, in a way Sara hadn't mastered without professional help. She was tall, elegant. Everything Sara was not. This woman's looks were a weapon she wielded.

She resembled the women she'd seen on Lance's arm in those tabloid photographs, and the ones that still showed up when she looked online, torturing herself with the untruths about their fake relationship. Initially she'd done it for amusement. To laugh at the fiction they wrote, because it was all a morass of lies. Which led her to contemplate the truth of what they wrote about Lance… But then there were the nastier comments. The talk of inevitable infidelity on his part, comparing her to his bevy of past lovers and finding her wanting in every way.

You'll never have his heart.

No, she wouldn't let the cruel memory taunt her. That didn't matter. He might not want her heart, but she didn't want Lance's either. All she wanted was his body. Didn't she? But that didn't deal with the woman in front of her, one brow raised in a supercilious way, almost tapping her foot, waiting for some response.

'Excuse me?' Sara asked.

The woman elegantly waved one hand in the direction of the field. 'Everyone wonders how you caught him. One moment he's the world's most wanted bachelor and the next, well, here we are.'

'Love's like that.'

'Love. *Of course.*' Said with disdain, as if Sara were some kind of fool. The woman took a healthy swig of her champagne and grabbed Sara's left hand. In the shock of the moment, Sara didn't have the wherewithal to pull away.

The woman glared at Sara's engagement ring, her lip curled in what appeared to be a triumphant smile. 'Pretty. But it's not the Astill Amethyst.'

As if that jewel had some kind of mythic status. How did this woman know about it? When had she been close enough to see it? A tightness clenched in her gut, hard and sickening, as if she'd drunk sour milk. Sara wanted to see it now too. Even though, had they been engaged for real, she still wouldn't have wanted it to grace her finger.

The woman looked impassive, cool and poised, like every woman she imagined Lance would spend time with. But it didn't matter. Lance had chosen this ring for her.

'Beautiful and complex, like you.'

That was *all* that mattered.

Sara plucked her hand from the woman's grasp. 'I don't have the amethyst because I loathe the colour purple.'

The woman's eyes barely widened a fraction. 'Really?'

The word was loaded with so much that was unsaid. That Sara was too unpolished. Too gauche for a man like the Duke of Bedmore.

'With the greatest of respect…' Sara knew the woman meant none '…we hadn't heard anything about you, and then here you are. From Lauritania as well. Everyone knows Lance despises the place.'

Enough. Sara straightened her spine, standing as tall as she could. Whilst her country had a multitude of failings, she still loved it. She'd been trained to be its *Queen.*

'Yes. Here I am. *Engaged.* With a sparkly ring and all.' She wiggled the fingers of her left hand in the woman's direction, feeling more petty than queenly.

The woman said nothing, merely turning back to the field, took another sip of champagne. Sara watched her gaze as it travelled over the players. Lance had removed his shirt. Sara was sure that was a scandalous thing to do, but the sight of his muscular back and the vee of his torso dried her mouth.

'He's a fine horseman. Do you ride?'

The wicked memory of her astride Lance, his head thrown back as she took him deep inside her flickered through her head.

'Horses?' Sara asked with feigned innocence.

That was greeted with a supercilious raised eyebrow. 'No. Do you?'

'Of course.' Sara had no doubt this woman would be perfect at everything she did. Unlike her. She was too unruly, too forthright. Too much of everything. 'I'm sure Lance will teach you. He's kind like that. But you do know what they say about him?'

'I'm sure if I don't you'll enlighten me.' A prickle of something cold ran down her spine.

'The Duke of Bedmore. Beds 'em, not weds 'em. Chucks 'em after he—'

'Play nicely, Vic.' That deep, soothing male voice. Lance. Relief coursed through her. She wheeled around and placed her hand on his chest, as much for the ice-cold beauty behind her as for anyone else in the crowd.

'Darling—' she said in a way that might have sounded a little too breathless and a lot too fake, but she didn't care '—you were outstanding. But I haven't been introduced to...' She waved her hand in the direction of the other woman in a dismissive manner, the perfect balance of queenly *and* petty this time.

The woman smirked, then downed the last of her champagne in one gulp. Lance frowned, but the look in his eyes was hard to fathom. Distant, sad. Lost.

'Sara, this is Lady Victoria Carlisle. My sister.'

'Your...sister?'

Of all the things she'd expected, that was not it. Victoria dumped her empty glass on a server's tray. Grabbed another. Took another healthy sip and raised her glass.

'Pleased to meet you. Welcome to the family. I look forward to the blessed union and so forth.' She turned to Lance with a brittle smile. 'See? I know how to play nicely.'

Lance took the glass of champagne from Victoria's hand and gently set it down on a side table before grabbing some water to hand to her instead. She pouted but accepted the glass and took a sip. That sadness was in her eyes too.

'Enough.' His voice was soft and low. He turned to Sara, cupped her face. Dropped his mouth to hers in a gentle kiss. 'I need to have a chat with my sister. Are you safe to entertain yourself for a few moments?'

Sara touched his hand. 'Of course.'

He turned and led his sister away. Something was going on, something painful to both of them.

Something terribly broken, in need of repair.

Lance took Victoria to a quiet corner, or as quiet as he could find in the marquee, where champagne flowed and people were a little the worse for wear. He checked her over as subtly as he could, because being late to the event usually meant she'd had an argument with her husband. He was relieved to see no bruises Vic would try to explain away. However, Lance knew bruises didn't have to be physical. The tongue could lash as mightily as a fist. Because she wasn't wearing sunglasses, he was able to check her eyes. Her pupils were a normal size today, not pinprick. Her voice was clear and cutting, not slurred. To his mild relief, Vic presented nothing other than a cool and brittle aristocratic demeanour.

'She's a pretty little thing.'

Lance hoped she hadn't been too cruel. His sister had a fine capacity to wound, honed to rapier-like precision. He missed the sweet, soft teenager she'd once been, until their parents had destroyed her life.

'Sara's *beautiful*.' And she was. In a dress the same pale blue as her eyes, she glowed. The way she'd looked at him as he'd dressed to ride had almost made him disgrace himself.

'Must be love.' Vic gave an unladylike snort. 'I didn't think our family believed in it. Girl has a spine too. She'll need that in—'

'Leave him.'

Vic's gaze shot to his, a little wide. She was an expert at hiding her emotions, but Lance could sense the fear nonetheless. The way she flinched as if under attack.

'Astills don't divorce.' The tone of her voice, those words, were a perfect imitation of their mother.

'You're not an Astill any more, so feel free. *Please.*'

Vic shook her head. 'I've got nothing. You don't understand.'

He hadn't protected her back then, but he could protect her now.

'I told you—'

'I'm not taking any of Father's money!'

Vic had always seen the inheritance as tainted. A poisoned chalice she would not touch. He had trouble understanding why, when what he had could help her.

'I'm not asking you to. I have my own. I can help.'

'And now I have to rely on the charity of my own brother? What would everyone say? Look at poor Victoria Carlisle. Barren… Divorced…'

'Vic, what hold does he have over you?'

She shook her head, her glass of water quivering in her fingers. 'Nothing you could ever understand.'

'I could try if you expl—'

'No. Leave this be. It's not your concern.'

Yet again, she wouldn't accept his help. Another failure to add to the litany of shortcomings in his past. Not only his sister, but Sara too. He'd meant to protect her, look after her, and what had he done? Taken her to bed. Touched her with fingers soiled by his genes, by generations of reprobates. Sara might look at him as if he were all things perfect, as if he were a god, but he couldn't shake the feeling that she would be tainted for ever by their association.

'I hope Victoria wasn't…difficult.' The car was warm in the autumn sunshine. They hadn't spent much longer at the post match celebrations. Seeing Vic had coloured the rest of the afternoon, relief and concern all tangled into one congealed mess of emotions.

'Is she often?' No denial then. Sara stared out of the window at the passing countryside.

'She's changed since she was a child.' It was as if he had to defend her against the cruelties the world had meted out. Ones he hadn't prevented. 'She was happy once.'

'And then she grew up.' The distant wistful sound of her voice said a great deal about Sara's current thinking. There was more in the loaded tone than a mere comment about his sister. 'What happened?'

'Her marriage isn't a good one.' That wasn't breaching any real confidence, but it so far underplayed what was going on there, he couldn't help the stab of guilt.

'Lots of people have unhappy marriages.'

'It was arranged, by my parents. To further my father's career. Mine too, if I'd wanted.'

His parents certainly had. His father had grand

plans for Lance. The House of Lords, politics, Prime Minister. Victoria had been the sacrificial lamb. He gripped the steering wheel even tighter.

Sara whipped round then, eyes slightly wide. *'Oh.'*

The way she stared at him said too much. As if she'd peered deep inside him and in some way found him wanting. She reached out her hand and placed it on his thigh, the touch warm and comforting. He wanted to shrug it off. He didn't deserve any respite. His sister had none.

'You can't save someone until they want to be saved.'

'I don't know what she wants,' he said. The pain of that recognition was unrelenting. At five years younger than him, Vic was too young for this life where she seemed to numb her sorrows in a bottle of painkillers. He knew she wanted children desperately. For whatever reason, no pregnancy had come, and each year he watched her fold into herself as if trying to disappear. With a cruel husband blaming her, rather than accepting some things might never be.

'She seems to care about you a great deal. She was only being protective.'

'That's no excuse.'

Another gentle touch of her hand. 'You don't need to apologise for something that's not within your ability to control.'

She was so wise, each word assuaging some of the pain that plagued him. It wouldn't last, it never did. The taint of guilt always crept over him. Like a slick of oil he could never wash free.

'The charity you were playing for...'

'Helping domestic violence victims.'

'Does Victoria have a particular interest?'

What could he say that wouldn't alert Sara to how much more to this story there might be? The terrible things he suspected.

'She seems to.'

Sara nodded. 'Then I shall make a donation. For her. To help.'

'Perhaps you might become friends.'

Or perhaps not. Victoria and Sara might be close to the same age, but Victoria had few friends now, seemingly trapped in a world of her own misery. Her only joy appeared to come from her horses, and the other wounded creatures she tried to rescue along the way.

'I don't believe I'm supposed to be around long enough.' Her voice was barely a whisper. What was he thinking? The truth was, he hadn't been. She flummoxed him, unsettled him, tangled his thoughts when he needed to keep them straight. Sara was short-term. His duty was to save her, set her on her feet and then set her free. Nothing more.

They drove the rest of the way in relative silence, even though he knew Sara had things to say. The way her gaze kept flicking to him. How she nibbled her bottom lip in contemplation.

They arrived at Astill Hall and he parked the car. He couldn't be around her. Those knowing looks, as if she wanted to *talk* about things. He couldn't deal with that. How would she feel if she discovered he hadn't protected his own sister?

So, telling Sara he had to go and tend to the horses, he went to the stables. He helped the groom rub them down, made sure they had no injuries. Once he'd satisfied himself, he went to his room, desire for Sara and disgust in himself congealing in a potent morass of emotion he needed to wash away.

He walked into the en suite bathroom and undressed, tossing his clothes on the floor. Turned on the shower, planted his hands on the wall and stood as the hot water rushed down his back. At least they'd raised over ten thousand pounds today. That would help alleviate some suffering. Assuage some guilt.

'May I join you?'

Her soft voice jolted him from his introspection. He straightened to say something, to say no, even as every part of him became hard and ready for her. Yet his words died in his throat when he turned.

Sara stood in the bathroom, glorious and naked, unruly hair round her shoulders, spilling to the tops of her breasts, her tan nipples beaded and tight, almost begging for his mouth to be on them. She didn't wait for an answer, stepping under the hot spray, her skin pinking as it splashed her. He should turn the temperature down, but she didn't complain, and he was too lost in her blue eyes to do anything but stare.

She reached out and ran her hands over his chest. Despite the heat of the water raining down on them, his skin shivered in goosebumps at her gentle touch. He should tell her to go, that he was dirty and he'd make her unclean too. Any moment now he'd say something…

'It looked rough today.'

'No more than normal,' he managed to grind out, though he wasn't sure she was speaking about his riding.

'I liked it…watching you. All that control. You were…impressive.' She looked down at him, erect and aching, the drops of water sparkling like raindrops on her eyelashes. 'No one could take their eyes from you.' She licked her lips.

He didn't give a damn if the whole world had been watching. All he cared about was the female perfection studying him now, as if he were her last meal.

'Wondering if I would elicit some scandal from the back of one of my ponies is all.' His voice sounded tight and strained, even to his own ears.

She ran her hands over his pectoral muscles and his breathing hitched.

'Did you hurt yourself?'

He couldn't say anything as her hand trailed down his abdomen, lower and lower, till he dropped his head back against the tiles. Then she stopped. He wanted to shout out, but all he did was shake his head.

'I want to check and make sure,' she said, and right now he'd agree to sign his soul over to the devil so long as she continued to caress every part of him. If he hadn't done so already, many years before.

She continued the soft touches on his arm, tracing it. Looking for what, he wasn't sure. A careful inspection of his skin. She placed her hand on his hip and applied enough pressure to tell him she wanted him to turn around. So he did, and she kissed him between his shoulder blades, her tongue licking at the water there before continuing her exploration, running her gentle, questing hands over his back. Down lower. Down each leg, and he knew—he *knew* she was on her knees.

He groaned. 'Sara.'

She stroked over a graze on his hip. Kissed it gently. Kissing him better.

'Turn round,' she murmured against his wet skin.

He hesitated for just a heartbeat before he complied. She was on the floor before him, looking up. Hair in wavy ribbons plastered to her body. Skin flushed pink all over. Mascara blurred and smudged. Little rivulets of water running down her face. She licked at one running over her lips and he almost lost himself then and there. Then her eyes left his face, looked at him, aroused in front of her. Took him in hand, and he bucked in her warm, steady fingers. She smiled then, like a siren.

'I think you like this.' All he could do was hiss as she tightened her grip and moved her hand like he'd shown her one night, when she'd asked how he enjoyed being touched.

He couldn't take his eyes from her. Her gaze was intent, her mouth so damned close he wanted to beg, to weep, and then the corners of her lips tilted. She moved closer still. Her mouth opened and her tongue licked the head of him. Then slowly, so slowly, she wrapped her lips round him and took him into her mouth.

She had him completely in her thrall. He would give her all the riches he owned, his heart, his soul, everything to ensure she'd never stop what she was doing now. He couldn't stop his hips from leaning into her and she moaned as if she was enjoying it, her eyes closed, wrapping her hand round him, gripping tight and working him till he didn't know who he was or what he wanted any more. Except her. Always craving her.

The base of his spine prickled. Any moment now he'd lose himself completely. He pulled out and she made a small whimper of protest.

'Up here,' he growled. Lance bent down, hands under her arms as she surged to his mouth, teeth clashing as she kissed him, wrapping her arms round his neck as he slammed her against the cool tiles. She lifted her leg and he gripped it, hauling her up his body with both hands under her backside, opening her to him. The panting of their breaths filled the room.

He angled himself, and the heat of her centre began to envelop him as he gave one hard thrust and entered her. She moaned long and low. Her nails scraped against his scalp, fingers gripping his hair. It stung as she tugged, but he relished the pain. Thrusting hard and deep, their bodies slapping and sliding against each other, grappling for purchase. That prickle in his spine started again, something heavy and unstoppable. Sara's legs tightened around his waist as her whole body clenched and spasmed round him. She tore her mouth from his and cried out, tumbling over the precipice. He followed with a roar echoing through the room.

He was spent, legs weak. The only thing keeping him upright was that he held Sara, and he didn't want her to fall, wouldn't let her go. He eased out of her, and she slid down his body, the water still streaming over him. Her lips were red as summer cherries, her body marred by finger marks and evidence of how rough he'd been. She'd wanted to check for his injuries, but he'd hurt her. He stroked his hand over the marks he'd left.

'You'll bruise.'

She smiled, a glorious sight with her bee-stung lips. 'I don't mind. I love your marks on me.'

Marks, they had consequences. A chill ran through him. Consequences. He hadn't worn a condom. He dropped his head to hers. 'No protection.'

She smoothed the hair from his face. Ran her hands over his chest. Was he ready for her again? His heart pounded. She made him insatiable. And, strangely, the fact that he hadn't worn a condom didn't trouble him as much as it should have.

'I'm on the pill and I assume…you've been checked?'

'I have.'

He took his health seriously, the reassurance of his partners even more so. And the secret truth was that, despite the tabloid chatter, he hadn't been with anyone for some time. And he'd *never* been with anyone unprotected.

She brought her lips to his. 'Then let's spend the rest of the afternoon in bed.'

His mouth descended on hers once more. Against his better judgement, he couldn't say no.

CHAPTER NINE

SARA CURLED UP in a chair in the bright parlour sipping coffee, shoes off, the sunshine warming the room. This was her favourite place in the house, with its yellow-papered walls adorned with little roses, overlooking the rose garden itself, which she'd been talking to the gardener about renovating to its former glory. And if this was her favourite room, then sitting with Lance after breakfast, as he attended to business whilst she looked on, was becoming one of her favourite pastimes. Small domestic moments that made her feel as if she belonged somewhere.

As he did every morning, Lance read the death notices. It seemed like a morbid enterprise, but he'd told her he was always looking to see who'd died and needed their estate *'picked over like a carcass'*. It was an odd thing to say when she found their hunting trips, as she now called them, exciting. She hadn't found anything like a Caravaggio, but she had identified some beautiful, valuable pieces which would hopefully do well at auction. Her parure had been sold. Soon she'd be completely independent of him, as she'd wanted.

She didn't know why that thought sat so heavily on her chest.

Sara took another sip of the rich, strong brew that the kitchen had perfected. She was sure her presence in Astill Hall was keeping Lance away from what he should be doing. His business was in London after all, but he didn't seem to mind being in the country. A complicated man in many ways, he kept so much hidden from her. Only in bed did he lay himself bare, and for those passionate hours she felt blessed. They'd settled into a kind of routine here, working together. Making love. Then when Lance was away, attending to duties around the estate, she'd explore the place herself.

'You'll get in trouble, looking at me like that.'

Lance's gaze hadn't lifted from his phone at all.

'How do you know I'm looking at you?'

He lifted his eyes, and something about them had changed, their appearance liquid and heated. 'I can always feel you looking at me.'

Lance dropped his mobile to the couch, stood and sauntered over to her with a lazy roll of his hips that made her think of a stalking predator.

'You're too far away.'

She put down her coffee and he swooped on her, swinging her into his arms. She laughed. 'Your tea will get cold. I know how you like it hot.'

'The only temperature I care about is yours.' He turned and walked back to his spot on the couch and sat with her nestled in his lap, nuzzling her neck with his lips, the warmth of his breath sending shivers through her.

'See?' he murmured against her overheating skin, as he trailed gentle fingers along her arm. 'Goosebumps. You need warming.'

He liked to play, she realised, take things slow, wind her higher and more frantic until she splintered, screaming his name loud. Right now, she didn't want slow. She wanted fast. As she straddled him, he slid his palms to her backside, dragging her forwards and flush against him.

His hardness nestled between her thighs.

'Yes.'

He raised an eyebrow, the corner of his lips quirked in a wicked smirk. Then she gave in to the impossible urge to rock against him. His eyes darkened to the colour of storm clouds before hail.

'You getting any warmer?' The words ground out of him as if he were battling for control. She was about to boil, as he cupped the back of her head and drew her to him, capturing her mouth, his free hand sliding up her thigh under the skirt of her dress. He brushed his thumb back and forth over her panties and she moaned.

'Much better than tea,' he murmured against her lips as she gave in to the burn of her body, chasing the sensation bearing down on her. 'That's it. I love you like this. Hot. Wet. Mine.'

His.

It should bother her. It really should. But if it troubled her enough she'd have to stop, and she couldn't. The feeling that she was melting like candle wax all over him was too delicious. Especially because she was there, almost there.

A bell softly chimed in the distance, or maybe it was in her head. She wouldn't be surprised if a chorus of angels started singing, this man brought her so close to heaven. She didn't care as their kisses deepened and he began unbuttoning the top of her dress with fervent fingers.

'Sir!'

She paused. Was that George's voice? She'd never heard him raise it.

'I won't be denied!'

Sara scrambled away from Lance as the protestations came closer. She knew that second voice, although she could hardly believe he was here.

'What the hell?' Lance muttered, adjusting himself and drawing the bodice of her dress together.

The door to the parlour smacked open as her brother stormed in, followed by Lance's butler, looking ready for a fight.

Lance straightened, all the heat bleeding out of him, replaced by something lazy and dangerous. The predator was back, and right now his gaze was fixed on someone Sara had never expected to see here.

'Really, George, why do people insist on disturbing us? Can't a man be the king in his own castle?'

'Your Grace, this man barged in. Would you like me to call the police?'

Her brother Heinrich stood stiff and to attention just inside the doorway.

Lance shook his head and waved in Heinrich's direction as if he were merely an annoying fly.

'Come back in five minutes. We could all probably do with more tea.' Then he glanced at her. 'Or, dare I say, a stiff brandy.'

George raised his eyebrows but backed out of the room and closed the door behind him. Sara clutched at the front of her dress, realising that in her haste she'd fastened the buttons in the wrong buttonholes. Her brother noticed. His scowl deepened.

He poked his finger towards Lance as if trying to punch a hole in the air. 'You!'

'Lance…' She tried to take a breath to calm herself, because the tremble of desire had been replaced by one of fear. 'This is my brother—'

'I know who it is.' Lance turned to her, his voice low, his eyes narrow and cold. Then he whipped back round to her brother, striding forwards with his hand out as if it was perfectly normal for Heinrich to be barging into their home. It was a complete change of demeanour.

'Hans! What a pleasure to greet you today as my brother-in-law-to-be.'

'Heinrich!' her brother hissed, looking at Lance's hand as if it were a snake and not a peace offering. He didn't reach out his own.

Lance ignored the slight, the disdain flicked off him as if it were water brushed away by wipers on a windscreen. Although, by the look of him, it wasn't peace he sought, standing tall and stiff with his jaw clenched.

'Henry, of course.' Lance turned to her and winked, his grin cocky and devilish. Heinrich's colour deepened to a shade of angry purple. Sara couldn't see what on earth was funny about this. Her brother had been trained in the military, an officer in Lauritania's small but efficient army. There was always a sense of suppressed violence about him, not so suppressed today.

'You're coming home, Sara.' Heinrich spoke in Lauritanian. It was an insult when Lance stood in the room. She refused to have a conversation with her brother that Lance couldn't understand.

'I don't think so. Since she's engaged to me,' Lance replied before she could say anything. He spoke Lauritanian? Her eyes widened and so did her brother's. 'Sara, I know I've never whispered sweet nothings to you in your native tongue. I was leaving that surprise to our wedding night.'

'Never.' Heinrich strode forwards, slashing his

hand through the air like a knife. She flinched. The way he looked at her, as if she were dust on his shoe and he was disappointed the polished leather was soiled. 'He will never marry you. It's all false.'

At least Heinrich had something right, though she'd never admit it. She couldn't say anything because she was a terrible liar. Sara wanted her brother gone, out of this house. The longer he stayed, the more he would taint the memories here.

'It's not false. I've put a ring on it, so to speak,' Lance said, standing straighter and taller, taking faux offence. 'One that's as precious and sparkling as Sara. The light of my life.'

He looked down at her, warm and kind, his eyes dancing with entertainment, and she smiled in return. She couldn't help herself. The man was simply too much.

Lance cupped her cheek. 'Ah. There it is. What I've been waiting for.' He smiled back, and the moment became something precious between them.

'Stop this fakery!' Heinrich shook his finger at Lance as if he were scolding. 'Sara, men like this only want one thing. He's using you and when he's done he'll cast you aside.'

Lance turned, mouth a thin line. 'Like your family used her?'

That stopped Heinrich in his tracks. His eyes widened. 'I have no idea what you're speaking of.'

'I'm talking about another convenient arrangement to shore up your family's power. This time to a man almost twenty years her senior, whilst she was still wearing mourning clothes. Since Sara's first fiancé inconveniently *died*.'

'You're besmirching my esteemed family when your own is such a disgrace, an utter blight on the aristocracy?' Heinrich fixed his cold, cruel gaze on her. 'Sara, you were destined to be Queen, and *this* is who you choose?'

Lance moved in front of her, shielding her from Heinrich's censure.

'I'm from one of the oldest families in the UK. Distantly in line for the throne, as Sara kindly reminded me before we announced our engagement. So you see, Harold, she's not really trading down.'

Sara hadn't spoken up enough in her life, and she didn't intend to be a coward now. She stepped to the side to see Heinrich and Lance glare at each other, like circling bulls pawing at the ground.

'I'm *not* going home,' she said, crossing her arms and trying to look resolute when her stomach churned in a sickening sensation. Her hands trembled. 'I've done my duty. I did it for years. Now is time for *me*. Go. I'm happy here.'

Heinrich sneered at her. 'You turn your back on the family and there will be *nothing* for you.

When this man casts you aside and you come fleeing home you'll be no more than the dirt on our soles.'

Even though she tried not to feel the pain of those words, they sliced sharp and true. She'd long suspected her only value to the family was in being sold off to the highest bidder. Today proved it.

Before she could say anything in response, the door opened and George walked into the room with a tray containing a teapot, a trio of cups and a bottle of brandy.

'Tea, Your Grace.' He placed it on a small side table. 'And brandy if so required. Do you need anything else?'

'Thank you. Please wait, I require a moment.' Lance's focus turned to Heinrich once more, his eyes the cold colour of a glacial moraine, hard and green. 'Say what you like about me, but you will *never* speak that way about Sara. George, where are the duelling pistols?'

Sara froze, as if the ice on the surface of Lake Morenburg had cracked and she'd plunged into the frigid waters beneath.

George remained ever the professional, completely impassive in the face of the drama surrounding him. Although his mouth might have twitched at the corners.

'Sadly, we have no ammunition. They haven't been used in two hundred years.'

Lance cocked an eyebrow. 'Hmm. That long?'

'With the greatest of respect, sir, you're not the finest shot.'

'But I am handy with a rapier.' Lance homed in on her brother once more, eyes full of deadly intent. 'Swords, then.'

Heinrich blanched. 'There will be no duelling.'

'You always were a coward. Unlike last time, there's no one to take your place today, so of course there will be duelling. Where are the rapiers, George?'

'Behind you, Your Grace. Would you like me to retrieve them from the cu—'

'No.' Lance stormed to a cupboard and thrust open the doors, frowning. Sara rushed to him, heart pounding. She had to stop this. Heinrich merely paced, clenching and unclenching his hands, muttering expletives all directed at her fake fiancé.

'Lance?' She placed her hand on his arm. His muscles tensed under her fingers. She didn't know what she wanted to say, other than to protect this man who was becoming precious to her in ways she couldn't even begin to contemplate right now. 'He was in the army. He fenced at school.'

'I know.' Lance's voice was hard as he withdrew two terrifying swords from the cupboard.

Thin, gleaming blades of steel. 'Your brother and I have a history with weapons like these. It'll be all right. I did fencing too. Don't let your brother dim your happiness. I might become truly angry if he causes that to happen.'

He wheeled round and thrust a hilt towards her brother. 'Take this, Henry.'

'*Heinrich!*'

'I know your name. I simply refuse to dignify you with it.'

'I will not fight.' Her brother clasped his hands behind his back. 'You are being ridiculous.'

Lance dropped the sword in his left hand, which fell to the floor with an ominous clatter. He lifted the other and pointed it, leaving the barest distance from Heinrich's chest. Her brother stiffened.

'Perhaps. Better a fool than a boor and a bully like you.' Lance's stance was lazy yet assured. He brought the blade forwards with a twist and flick. A button flew from her brother's shirt. 'Like the Crown Prince.' Flick. Another button. 'May he rot in hell.' Flick. And another. 'You knew he wasn't faithful to Sara, that he'd never protect her, or love her. Yet you criticise me for *imagined* failings, when yours are very *real* and caused her harm?'

Heinrich stood, marble-white, the same colour as his ruined shirt. Lance stalked forwards, rapier at his side, bringing his own face mere inches from her brother's.

'Before I give you a scar to match my own, run along home like the coward you are.' Lance's hand gripped the sword tight, his knuckles pale.

'You're afraid for your own reputation, not for your sister. But remember, your King is my best friend. Whilst Sara is with me she'll have the full force of his protection, not to mention your Queen's. So take that back to your family, and choke on your aristocratic pride along with it.'

Lance turned his back on her brother, eyes blazing and fierce, like a golden warrior as he focused only on her.

'George, before I do something ill-advised,' he hissed through gritted teeth, 'please throw him out.'

Somewhere, far away in the house, the front door slammed. Heinrich hadn't waited to be escorted from the house, storming out on his own. Sara's whole body slumped in relief. She walked to Lance, his jaw still clenched, all hard and ferocious. She wanted to throw herself into his arms, be held, but by the look of him he wouldn't welcome it.

'What did Heinrich do to you?' she asked, her voice trembling as she tried to control the leftover ripple of fear still coursing through her.

Lance handed his sword to George, who collected the other from the floor and left the room with them.

'We both fenced at school. Heinrich was good, but I was better and he *hated* it. Hated Rafe and I, as all the boys at the Kings' Academy did. One day he challenged me to a fight with rapiers he'd smuggled from home.' Lance clenched his hands then flexed his fingers. 'I don't believe he thought I'd go through with it, but I wouldn't back down. When the time came he claimed to have injured his wrist. Said *I* was the coward if I refused to fight the person who'd offered to take his place. The school champion.'

Sara lifted her hand, then hesitated. The tightness around Lance's eyes softened as she stroked her fingers over the fine scar on the side of his jaw.

'You received this.'

'They wanted to draw blood. Teach me a lesson. It was never a fair fight. Fortunately, a teacher caught us. The school sought to hush up the whole mess. I suspect your family did too, given my father's carefully cultivated friendship with the King. Luckily for me, the blade was sharp and Lauritania had some fine plastic surgeons.'

Sara shook her head. She'd suspected her brother could be devious and cruel, but she'd had no idea what had happened all those years ago at school. There'd not been a hint of it at home.

'Thank you. For seeing him off.'

'I'll do *anything* to keep you smiling.' His voice was a tortured rasp. 'But be warned. I'm no one's hero.'

'You may not think so, but you're a hero to me.'

His nostrils flared, his lips a tight line. It was as if he was still looking for a fight, after her brother's inaction.

'Come with me,' he said. 'There's somewhere I haven't shown you.'

Lance stalked to the door and thrust it open. She hurried to catch up as he made his way through long halls, past room after grand room she'd not yet explored.

'Where are we going?' Her breaths huffed as she attempted to match his long stride. Still he didn't slow down, as if driven by some imperative to keep moving.

'You'll see.'

Lance kept up his relentless pace until they reached the southern side of the house, entering a long room with a rich red carpet. A bank of windows to the right overlooked a stretch of emerald grass that collided with a planted woodland. Scattered through the space were a few plush chaises facing a vast wall of portraits. Lance stopped, turned to the pictures and swept his arm wide.

'I'd like to introduce you to my illustrious family,' he said, his lip curled almost in a sneer.

She stared at the array of pictures. They seemed

the same as the Morenburg Palace portraits, and those of her own family home. The aristocracy cataloguing their imagined magnificence for all to see.

'Why bring me here?'

'You should meet some of my ancestors.' Lance paced restlessly before stopping at an impressive gilt-framed portrait of a man dressed in scarlet trimmed with ermine, his robes bejewelled with pearls and rubies, elegant hand at his waist, one finger touching a golden key hanging from his belt.

'The Fourth Duke of Bedmore, an incurable hedonist. There's nothing he wanted that he didn't acquire. Married the beautiful young Mary to get himself an heir, then made it his mission to strip her considerable fortune.'

Sara studied the portrait. Its subject was handsome, even to the modern eye, standing with a familiar, almost amused look on his face.

'That's how things were then. I don't think many in the aristocracy married for love.'

Lance didn't acknowledge her, entirely focused on the painting. 'Mary was said to be desperately unhappy. She'd been meant for another man, but the Duke made certain promises to her and she fell for them. As did her family. Sound familiar?'

Sara shrugged. 'It's nice to think in some ways things have changed.'

'Have they?' Lance wheeled round, raising a sardonic brow. 'When he tired of Mary he locked her in her apartments. Demanded servants pass food through a barred door he refused to open. Would release her on rare occasions, only if she "behaved", and who the hell knows what that meant? He's smiling. This portrait shows his hand on the only key to her chambers. For years the portrait was kept in her sitting room, above the fireplace. A *reminder* to her of what he could do if he wanted to. That there was *no one* to stop him.'

Sara's breath caught, a sickening sensation twisting inside her as recognition flowed through her. Had her own life been much different? Engaged to a man who'd only wanted her pedigree, her ability to bear his heirs. Parents who hadn't cared that Ferdinand was unfaithful, their only response the cold reminder that she'd marry, become Queen and do her duty. Whilst she hadn't been locked in a tower, she'd been trapped nonetheless...

'That's horrible.' She was unsure whether the words were for Mary or herself.

Lance jabbed his finger at the wall, continued describing a litany of his family's sins, not sparing the past Dukes in any way. He was right. They had all been drinkers, gamblers, adulterers and fornicators, as he'd warned months ago. Some of them had been even worse. When he came to the last portrait, his own, he stopped.

'That's my *history*, Sara. There was not a shred of good in any of my ancestors.' He shook his head. 'Don't ever call me a hero when there's ample evidence that I'm as bad as the rest.'

She must realise now. There was no way she couldn't when faced with the evidence of his family's infamy. Chasing off Sara's brother had been no heroic act. It was the *least* he could do; any other man would have done the same for her.

Yet rather than look at him with distaste, she cocked her head, placed a hand over her heart. 'Both of our families, even Lauritania's royal family, have profited from the misery of others. Do you think I'm immune? I haven't examined my past in detail, but there's ugliness there too. All we can do is try to be better.'

Lance ran his hand through his hair. 'You don't understand.'

He had to make her, for her own good.

'I do. You say you're a bad man. But you can't control my thoughts.'

She was achingly beautiful, in a blue dress covered with little roses. The portraits of his ancestors were at her back, the ghosts of his past watching them. It was time to show her the truth of being an Astill. The Eighteenth Duke of Bedmore. He'd spent most of his adult years cultivating the role, slipping into it with ease because, no matter what she thought of him, it was who he was born to be.

'What if I wanted us to continue what was interrupted earlier? Here. Now. Told you to strip from your dress with the eyes of my ancestors upon you.'

Her mouth opened. Closed. Pink bloomed on her cheeks. Then she began to stroll towards him with a sultry roll of her hips, her fingers working the buttons on the front of her dress, one after the other. He wanted to shout at her to stop, all the while silently begging her to continue.

Sara shrugged the dress from her shoulders, the fabric sliding over her body to the floor as she stepped out of it and stopped in front of him, wearing nothing but sheer blue lace underwear. Desire mingled with the remnants of his anger, a potent mix that scorched through him with blazing heat.

'I'm not afraid of the dead, Lance. They can't hurt you.'

She glowed in the light pouring through the windows, the angel he'd called her in every way. A sickening burn of disgust rose to his throat. He couldn't do this, not here in the presence of his cursed past. Not to her. He closed the distance between them and wrapped his arms round her, burying his head in the side of her neck, drinking in the intoxicating scent of her like redemption.

Sara sank into him with a sigh and the fury of the morning bled away. Lance swung her into his arms. He was damned if he'd let anyone hurt her. She should be cherished. He could do something right—he would prove it. He'd look after her till the time came for her to leave.

Even though he feared the person he needed to protect her from most was himself.

CHAPTER TEN

LANCE SAT IN his study, looking over the books. Everything had run seamlessly until now, with this pretence that he was leaving bachelorhood behind him. Who knew being a proper duke took so much work? His workload had seemed to increase exponentially since his pretend fiancée had entered his life. Or perhaps they were simply the demands of his staff trying to make things perfect for Sara, because she'd become beloved by them all.

Now George had given him some sort of report about Astill Hall. He'd never had a report about the particulars of running the house before. He trusted his staff implicitly to do their jobs, and nothing they'd ever done had caused him to question them. But George had insisted, inundating him with information about meals and things which needed to be done on the estate. The place was becoming unrecognisable. His efficient butler had tried to involve Sara in their meeting this morning, but Lance had refused. There was no need to disturb her when she was somewhere else about the house, probably in the kitchen garden with the chef, talking about vegetables.

It was all so domestic. The pleasure of that observation slid through him till he beat it away. What on earth was he thinking? Not much, bar the satisfaction of having her here. The house, which had been a mausoleum, causing him to spend most of his time in the bright lights of London, was beginning to feel like a home again. Every night spent together, limbs entwined. There was no pretence any more, the Duchess suite now unused unless they wanted a change of venue. It was all too satisfying, too comfortable. Yet… Once that might have given him an itch, now he gloated about it all. Life with Sara felt like something gloriously never-ending.

Except it had to end. The mere thought raised a howl deep inside him. But what was he, if not a man of his word? Still, her smile over coffee in the morning, glimpses of her as she explored the house and garden, set his heart alight. Perhaps he was selfish, but right now he didn't care.

Then he felt the glimmer of something. A sensation that spoke of a future which was concrete and permanent. The feeling of solidity he wanted to nurture and keep, not crush and destroy. He let it unfurl inside him, a far more interesting idea than listening to the cost of polishing the bloody chandeliers, which George was now discussing with him. As if he needed to know. But since Sara had entered the house it seemed the staff took their obligations of accountability terribly seriously. And rather than talking about said chandeliers and their repair he wanted to find her. Perhaps take her to their room, peel off whichever pretty dress she wore today. Make her gasp his name. Of course it didn't really need to be in their room.

He stared at the gleaming surface of the desk he was sitting at. Couldn't get out of his head the memory of Sara splayed out for him on the desktop, skin flushed, the glorious taste of her on his lips as she writhed under his tongue. Really, this room was no longer a place of work but a playground for his fantasies. And he had plans for every flat surface of his home. A dinner for two in the grand dining room, where he'd lay her out on the table and—

'You're not listening to a word I say.'

Could George imagine what might have been distracting him? Perhaps. He was canny like that. The man had been with him for years.

'No. You can do what you want with the chandeliers. You always have. Why now?'

'Lady Sara was raised to be a queen.' How much better would the Duchess of Bedmore sound? *Perfect.* And where had that thought come from? He shut it down. George went on. 'She will have high expectations, and all of us at Astill Hall are determined to exceed them.'

'I think she's merely happy to be here. I don't believe she has any expectations.'

Though Lance wasn't sure. Was she happy? He wanted her to be. It seemed imperative to discover whether she was. Immediately.

'Perhaps I should find Lady Sara and ask her?' George asked.

Lance gave a wry smile. 'Not if I find her first.'

His butler gave a knowing smile in return. 'If I may say—'

'Nothing's stopped you before.'

George cleared his throat. 'You've done well. Sara is a delight. We, all of us, are genuinely happy for you. It's a pleasure to have her in the house. And we've been wondering, would you like us to resurrect the nursery?'

'The *what*?'

The words were almost strangled in his throat. Except the thought of the nursery with a cot and mobile and pretty wallpaper didn't fill him with dread as he thought it should. He rubbed at an ache in his chest that felt something like yearning. For little cherubs like her. Hell, he couldn't be going there. But now his mind was filled with a vision of Sara, belly round with his child, sitting in the nursery in a rocking chair, nursing a baby. Of them running through the once silent halls, chasing squealing children. Little angels like herself. Those visions he'd had on the plane, as they were flying over here mere weeks before, coming back with a vengeance.

They made him glow with a satisfying heat, rather than cringe with cold dread. He should put an end to this talk, but somehow he couldn't. The words wouldn't come out to stop what he knew was foolishness and fantasy.

'Perhaps you should ask Sara what she'd like to do.'

There, he'd leave it with her and shut down these unfamiliar feelings. She'd tell George to wait, and that would be the end of that.

Lance stood, and his phone began to ring. He frowned. 'It's Victoria. I have to take it.'

George nodded and left the room as Lance picked up the phone.

'Vic. How are you?'

'Lance…' The sound was hollow with a slight delay, as if she was far away, her voice quiet and uncertain. 'It's only a quick call to let you know. I'm not allowed to talk for long.'

Allowed. A prickle of concern marched down his spine.

'Where are you?'

'Switzerland. A…a…clinic. Bruce thought it best.'

Hearing those words was like being thrown from his polo pony. The shock, then landing with a bone-jarring thud. That husband of hers, he'd never thought of what might be best for Vic. Ever.

Only himself and his career. Even if it crushed Vic in the process.

'Why? What's happened? Why is it best?'

'I need some time.' Her voice was so tired, as if all the life had leached out of her. She'd been such a vibrant young woman, once a bright and shining light like Sara. Then she'd married and everything had dimmed.

'Mother agrees. Bruce is going through a lot at the moment, what with the campaign and my inability to fall pregnant, and I'm...'

Politics. Parents and a man who didn't cherish his wife.

'It takes two to make a baby, Vic. That's not your fault.'

'It was.' Her voice was knotted and choked. 'The fall. You know it did something.'

She'd been in intensive care with internal injuries after an incident involving one of her rescued horses, and all anyone could worry about was whether she'd be able to get pregnant when she recovered. As if she were some brood mare and not a young woman to be loved and cherished.

He clenched his fists tight and gritted his teeth till he managed to hiss out the words, 'That was an accident. No one's fault. You could have IVF.'

'Nothing's worked and I'm tired. So tired.'

'You're not happy. I'll say it again. Take your chance now. I'll help you. *Leave him.*'

'But the horses. My other animals. They're…' It was what she didn't say. She was more afraid for the pets she loved than she was for herself. 'You know how Bruce feels. If I'm not there…'

Was that what he held over her? No, there had to be something else, something Vic wouldn't tell him. Lance didn't care any more. He would gather every animal she owned, make sure they were safe. Then he would bring her here. Bring her home.

'I'll come and get you. You can stay with me.'

'*No.* You're engaged now.'

'That doesn't matter.' *Nothing* mattered, apart from doing what he should have done in the beginning—protect her.

He heard the murmur of a voice in the background and the muffled sound of Vic's reply, as if her hand was over the phone.

'I've got to go. I won't be able to talk for a while. They say I need no contact with anyone. I'll call you when I can, but—'

'Wait! Vic. What's—'

'It'll be fine, Lance. I promise. I…love you.' Her voice cracked. 'It'll *all* be fine.'

The line went dead. He closed his eyes, taken back to that damn cathedral. She'd looked so beautiful and fragile walking down the aisle in her wedding dress, and he *knew* he should have grabbed her then, stopped the wedding. But he'd been too tied up in his own life to listen to his gut feeling and now here she was—far away from home, in some prison of a clinic where she wasn't even allowed to use a phone. The embarrassing wife being locked away by her husband whilst he campaigned. Who the hell knew what would happen to her there? All because of his failure to act.

The reality lay before him, stark and endless. He knew how to throw legendary parties; he knew countless ways to make a woman scream in pleasure; he knew what the tabloids wanted to hear to keep him on the front page. But he didn't know how to look after a woman, how to protect her. He couldn't protect anything or *anyone*.

His selfishness and thoughtlessness would destroy everything in the end. No one should ever place their care in his hands. Especially not another bright and beautiful young woman, one with her whole life ahead of her.

Again, all he could selfishly think about was Sara, barefoot and pregnant, in his house. But why? She probably didn't even want that. She'd been engaged to that man since birth. She didn't need to be trapped by another. His failures had ruined Vic. He couldn't be trusted. He'd ruin Sara too. And if he did that he'd never forgive himself.

Sara stood in the portrait gallery once more. She adored the whole house, enjoying her daily explorations when they weren't out working, or if

Lance wasn't corralling her against the nearest flat surface to undress her and make her scream his name. Frankly, not satisfied till she did.

Egotist.

She loved it. Was addicted to it. Addicted to him.

And yet here was where she came to ponder the man she'd slowly and inexorably fallen in love with, despite her best efforts. The whole of her existence in the house, the clear lines she'd set for herself, were blurred and smudged like a pastel picture.

She stared at the portraits before her. A gallery of his ancestors, stretching the length of the long wall. She'd studied them one by one, trying to figure out the family, endeavouring to understand *him*. This morning George, Lance's highly efficient butler, had come to her, asking about refurbishing the *nursery*. That wasn't the issue so much; the staff all came to her now with questions about Astill Hall, her preferences. As if she, not Lance, ruled the home. Assumptions made by the ring on her finger.

No, it was that *Lance* had directed him to talk to her.

When George had asked the question, she'd blushed. After what they'd done together, Lance completely unabashed and comfortable in himself and, in turn, making the passions of her own body come alive, the talk of a nursery and the prospect of babies made her flush red. Embarrassed like the virgin she well and truly wasn't any longer.

But a *nursery*. What did it mean? Lance could have answered that question with a short, sharp *no*. Yet he'd instructed George to seek her out, as if it were her decision. As if it was a question he wanted her to answer for him. And that answer whispered in her ear seductively.

Yes.

The breath was jagged in her throat. That couldn't be the answer. It really, truly couldn't. Yet the idea of him, of her, together in this house, a real marriage and children, spoke to her louder and louder. She hadn't meant for this to happen. All she'd wanted was freedom, and yet something about the fake situation she'd walked into felt all too real. It was a reality she didn't want to walk away from.

Because she felt free with Lance.

So she'd said yes. And George had smiled and practically skipped on his way. Which had led her here, to the gallery of Lance's ancestors, trying to figure him out.

She strolled down the line of paintings to his portrait. Each one sent a message, but his... If she didn't know better, she'd say it screamed a kind of warning. His picture made no pretence of dignity. The man in the portrait lounged, dissolute, almost

indecent, as if a lover had just left him. Shirt half open, a lazy gleam in his eye, a smirk on his lips. Looking louche and untrustworthy, bent on destroying everything formal, right and proper. It was an exquisite picture that had her standing in front of it far too long and too often. Because it was all irony, a joke on everyone who looked at it and only saw what they wanted to see.

She knew he wasn't the man in the painting, but someone else entirely. A man who cared for those who couldn't care for themselves. Someone serious, who hid his true self behind a veneer of humour and carelessness that he wore like a layer of ice over a lake, leaving everyone unaware of the depths beneath.

A man she craved to learn with every atom of her being.

'You spend too much time here.'

She whipped round. She hadn't heard him come in behind her because she was too absorbed by the picture. Lance leaned against a wall, arms crossed, jaw hard and somehow disapproving. Seeing him in the flesh eclipsed the picture. He was life, a force of nature that made everything else pale to sepia. But catching her out like this embarrassed her in a way she couldn't explain. How many times had he witnessed her here, staring, trying to figure him out because the real man confused her?

'Why do you say that?'

'My ancestors could corrupt by their pictures alone.'

'You are not the man in that painting.'

'Yes, I am. I'm exactly that man, and you'd be wise to remember it.'

Sara shook her head. She wouldn't be cowed. Never again.

'You like to pretend not to care. The problem is you care *deeply*. About the village, the estate… Your sister.'

Me. She hoped he cared about her.

'Angel, I'm good at pretending to have an interest when I don't, in anything much other than myself.' His voice sounded like a sneer, and she hated that he used the word *angel* like a weapon rather than a term of endearment. 'However, I don't wish to pretend any longer.'

'What do you mean?' She didn't understand any of this, but the look on his face terrified her. It was detached, cool. Not the heated way his eyes usually flared when they looked at each other.

'I'll be travelling to look at some horses, then I'm off to Switzerland.'

None of this had been scheduled in the obsessive diary he kept, the one he'd shared with her. This had to be new.

'Does this have anything to do with Victoria?'

His eyes widened almost imperceptibly, then

settled back into the lazy, bored charm he always fooled others with. Never her. Until now.

She didn't like it.

'George, I presume?' He raised a supercilious eyebrow.

Yes, George had told her in cautious tones that Victoria had called. As if she'd need to repair the damage after the conversation was done. But nothing appeared irreparably broken. Yet.

'He really oversteps the line,' Lance said. 'This has nothing to do with my sister, and everything to do with the future.'

Her heart rate spiked. 'Did he overstep in asking me about the nursery?'

Lance's brow furrowed to a frown, before smoothing again.

'He did say you suggested he talk to me,' she said.

Lance shrugged, a lazy nonchalance tainting him. 'It doesn't matter now.'

She wouldn't let that stand. She'd spent so much of her life accepting what was handed to her. Now she wasn't afraid to fight for what she wanted. If she didn't, who would?

'What if it matters to me? What if I told him yes, that the nursery should be refurbished?'

She held her breath as Lance's face shuttered, entirely devoid of emotion.

'I'd say it was a mistake. You want love. We know that's something I don't do.'

The words sliced to the heart of her, sharp and true, as she was certain they were meant to.

'You'll never—' No. She wouldn't let that voice intrude again. Sara ignored his words and focused on how he'd treated her, his actions. He'd been so kind, protective. Passionate. All he'd done for her over the weeks she'd been here told her that Lance felt something for her. But she suspected he didn't believe he was a good man, that he was capable of softer feelings.

'Are you sure? Some things here felt very much like love to me.'

'That's sex. Which has nothing to do with love.'

'But what we have—'

'Is chemistry. You've confused that with something deeper. So let me be explicit...'

He was disavowing her. Her mouth dried, her heart pounding frantically in her chest.

'Don't. Don't demean this. Us.'

He raised an eyebrow, his expression disdainful. As if she were a silly little girl who needed educating. 'I'd never demean sex. I'm an enthusiastic supporter, as you must have learned. But sex with a person is like your favourite meal. You might love it, but eat too much and you'll get bored eventually, and want to try something different.'

The impact couldn't have been worse if he'd taken a rapier and sliced her off at the knees.

'You're…bored of me?'

'You're an intelligent, charming young woman, but…' He shrugged her off as if she were nothing.

'You'll never have his heart.'

Of course. She'd been a fool to think this had meant anything. She took a deep breath, battling the burn in the back of her nose, the prickle in her eyes. She wouldn't cry. Not with all his wicked ancestors witnessing her misery.

'I thought…' She let the words trail off because she was really talking to herself. Lance didn't care. All along he'd treated this like a huge game, when she'd thought he was trying to make her smile, to chase away her sadness. Instead, he was probably mocking her. And, like with Ferdinand, she'd ignored the truth, hoping and dreaming that this could be something more, when she'd been nothing but a few moments' entertainment for a bored rich man.

He swept his arm wide. 'Yes, all of this gallery is filled with shysters and conmen who encouraged people to think and dream things they shouldn't. But, if you remember correctly, I never encouraged you with any false hopes.'

No, he hadn't. He hadn't encouraged her at all. He'd never whispered quiet words of love as he'd worshipped her body. He'd made no promises for the future. And she'd fooled herself into believing things because she was desperate for love. The trap she'd told herself she wouldn't fall into again.

'And now for my trip,' he said, and all she wanted to do was scream at him to be quiet, put her hands over her ears because she didn't want to hear any more.

'Please feel free to stay here for as long as you choose. I'm unlikely to be returning in the near future. My home is usually in London, after all.' Sara barely heard the words. They'd made love this morning, and now this? 'Astill's Auctions will pay the commission on your finds and will provide you with introductions to some of the finest auction houses in Europe, if you wish to find a job at any of them.'

Her humiliation was complete. He was paying her off like someone cheap and disposable. She wouldn't take it. She couldn't.

'I don't want your money, or your help.'

Lance flinched, before settling back into his cool, businesslike demeanour.

'It's what you deserve.' Money. Not love. *Never* love. 'You're exceptional at what you do.'

Sara couldn't let him see how much this hurt. How it wounded her to her soul. Deeply, irrevocably. She'd known the first moment she'd set eyes on him that he was trouble. Yet she'd sought him out, chased it. Well, she was reaping the tainted rewards of their liaison now. She looked down at her finger, to the opal there. *Beautiful and complex.* It burned, as if taunting her with what might have been. She wanted to tear it off. Instead, she carefully slipped it from her finger.

'You should have your ring back.' She held it out. He merely clasped his hands behind his back, staring at the exquisite piece as if it meant nothing at all.

'Keep it. If I were truly getting engaged I would have given my fiancée the Astill Amethyst.'

She felt like a fool now, standing there with the ring in her fingers, as if begging him to take it. She'd beg for nothing from a man ever again. She clenched the jewel in the palm of her hand when all she wanted to do was hurl it at him. But it represented something precious, a fleeting moment when she'd *believed* she was worthy. She wouldn't treat it with the disdain he'd shown her...

'I don't *need* it. I want nothing of yours. I can make my own way.'

'That, I don't doubt.'

She closed her eyes for a moment, holding back the tears she refused to allow to fall. He might claim not to doubt her, but in this moment she doubted everything. No. Not any more. No relying on others when she should find her own way, no relying on men to steer her course, letting her life be run by them.

It was time to be on her own, because she realised now she would have given Lance everything and left nothing of herself.

'I'll leave this afternoon.' She'd been raised to be a queen, to control her emotions. She would not let this overcome her. 'I've clearly outstayed my welcome and I shall leave you to your life.'

'There's no—'

Sara held up her hand. She mustered all the cold disdain he'd shown to her. 'Let's not be any more of a disappointment, shall we? How's this as a new moniker, Lance—the Disappointing Duke? I think it has quite the appeal.'

She turned, straightened her spine as her royal training had taught her and walked away from the man she'd thought she loved, the old diamonds of her engagement ring cutting into her palm as she did so.

CHAPTER ELEVEN

SARA WANDERED THE damp cobbled streets of Morenburg old town after the end of an early shift at the palace. She drifted through the antique markets on the way to her apartment. Sadly, on this dreary late-autumn day, they held no interest. A shard of pain sliced through her, a reminder of the things she tried to forget. On most days it was more like a bruise, dull and deep. But here, amongst all the sellers and the antiques and people looking for treasure, the universe liked to remind her of what she'd lost.

The breeze picked up, cutting into her. A distracting kind of sensation prickled the back of her neck. She wrapped her coat more tightly round her to ward off the chill. It seemed colder than normal. The rest of the crowd bustled round her, people laughing, going about their lives. Her life seemed permanently on hold now, when in truth she was *trying* to move forwards, after moving back home with a healthy bank balance and little more, to a country which didn't feel like hers any longer.

She'd left home behind in a person, not a place.

Now, everything reminded her of a man she couldn't have. A man who, she'd come to realise, after days of sobbing and self-recrimination, didn't love himself enough to love her the way she deserved. Sara had taken a while to accept that certainty. After his cruelty to her, pushing her away only hours after it seemed as if he wanted her closer. None of it had made sense, except that vicious voice in her head that told her she'd never have his heart. But after time away other memories apart from those of that awful last day invaded her consciousness.

How he'd protected her. How he worried for his sister. His staff, who loved him even if it didn't seem he could reciprocate. The villagers who spoke of his enduring care and kindness. How he'd always tried to keep her smiling, even when she'd wanted to curl into a ball and weep. If she could ignore his cruel words, that she was now sure had been designed to force her away, his had been the *actions* of a good man. The truths others believed were self-evident, Lance couldn't see for himself. That he simply wasn't the Dastardly Duke he pretended to be.

And in the end her heartbreak became more about his loss than hers. If Lance couldn't accept that he was a good man with the capacity to love, he'd never accept it from someone else. Having experienced being in love, Sara couldn't imagine now living without it in her life. But sadly, two months after she'd walked away from Astill Hall, she still had trouble contemplating her world without Lance in it. Still, some things you couldn't have, no matter how much you wanted them…

She sighed. There was no point to these ruminations. Not any more. Sara made her way through the milling crowds, past a kitschy tourist shop selling royal memorabilia. She hesitated. Little Lauritanian flags adorned the window, pictures of the still new yet quickly beloved King and Queen adorned random items on display— mugs, eggcups, tins of sweets. Then there were items commemorating the deceased King, Queen and Crown Prince, the past and the present colliding. One of those portraits could have been her, and she didn't even have a twinge of loss at the thought of what might have been. That sense of lost opportunity was for another person entirely.

A shadow passed her shoulder. Another prickle of awareness, this time hinting someone was close. Even though she'd tried to melt into obscurity, people still saw her as a minor celebrity here. The death of her fiancé and failed fake engagement meant she was a kind of tragic heroine. The woman who would have been Queen, still looking for love.

Sara took a deep breath, pasted a smile on her face. Prepared herself for the questions from a public that was mostly caring, if not sometimes intrusive. She looked up and glimpsed a tall, broad reflection in the glass of the shop window that choked the breath from her lungs.

'Ferdinand really was a fool, and not the only one.'

That voice. Her knees buckled, before she firmed them, her heart tripping then pounding. She took a long, steadying breath. It should probably have been no surprise that he was here. She'd heard the rumour that he was back in the country, had known he was working with the royal family, auctioning unwanted items from the palace, since the country's finances had been in a shockingly bad state and Lise and Rafe had been fighting to restore the economy.

'It's wrong to speak ill of the dead,' she said. Part of her craved a glimpse of him in the flesh, and another part knew she should leave well enough alone. But it was as if everything around her had stopped. The cold breeze, the sounds of people going about their lives. In this moment there was only her and him, as if the universe was waiting. And she couldn't ignore Lance any longer.

She turned, forgetting the full force of him.

He looked as heart-stopping as she remembered. More so. The curve of his bottom lip that had obsessed her for so long, had haunted her dreams. The green eyes that seemed to peer into the very soul of her. His jaw, now shaded with fashionable stubble. A man who knew more of her secrets, her desires, than any person alive.

But it didn't matter. He'd been clear that they had no future together, and she deserved more from life, someone who could love her with his whole heart, even if right now she couldn't contemplate loving anyone at all. Other than Lance, of course. But part of her hated him too, for playing on her fears. For having made her believe, once again, that she was something *less*. Before she'd realised that she had a future and a value.

That she was enough.

'I'm only speaking the truth. You know I can be cruel. Whereas you're too kind.'

Today he was dressed as if for business, standing there in a dark coat over a suit. No tie, the neck of his perfect bespoke shirt open, showing a tantalising hint of his chest, a sprinkling of hair. She was taken back to the times when she'd rested her head there, listening to the thump of his comforting heartbeat as it lulled her to sleep.

'It's not a bad thing to be kind, but it can be misplaced.' She shrugged. 'I think you believed the greatest act of kindness was your cruelty.'

'The Despicable Duke.' His eyes tightened, but otherwise his face remained blank. 'I told you they were right.'

He still underestimated himself, perhaps always would. And no matter how much she'd wanted a future with him, there would be none so long as he pitched himself as a bad man. Because in his mind he'd never truly deserved her love.

She shook her head.

'Still trying to find the good in me?' he asked.

'That's not my question to answer.'

It was whether he could find some good in himself that was important.

'Some would call me irredeemable, for things I've said.'

The breeze in the little lane picked up, a few late autumn leaves skittering about their feet. His words to her in their final conversation still pricked at her consciousness. He'd wanted her to walk away without a thought of turning back. He'd ensured it. So why did she crave to run to him and hope he caught her now?

She wrapped her arms round her waist, needing to leave but fixed to the spot. She looked towards the exit of the lane, anywhere except Lance. In the distance a small group began drifting down towards the tourist store.

'I should have thought you'd be happy with that. Your reputation soiled even more than before. Isn't that what you were trying to achieve?'

'Once, perhaps…'

A couple of people looked from her to him, as though in recognition. She didn't want this to become some spectacle, but didn't want to walk away either. She'd dreamed about seeing him, about what she'd say, since shortly after she'd left his house. Strangely, now it was as if her tongue was tied in knots. Then the truth began screaming loudly at her. Even after everything, she still didn't want an end. She wanted a beginning.

Lance frowned as someone in the crowd raised their phone as if to take a photograph. He turned his back on them and manoeuvred himself so any view of her was blocked by his height and breadth.

'Whilst I deserve public humiliation, you don't. Is there somewhere we could talk in private?'

Two equally tempting answers, yes and no, pitched a battle inside her. It was a terrible position to be in, wanting to toy with fire but not wanting to be burned.

'Are you going to be cruel to me again?' She tried to sound firm, but her voice was quiet and cracked.

He shut his eyes for a brief moment and flinched as if in pain. When he opened them again the intensity and heat in his gaze almost incinerated her on the spot.

'*Never.*'

That one simple word ground out of him with vehemence.

She was like Icarus, hurtling directly into the sun. She didn't care about the consequences. In the end, the side of her entirely disinterested in self-preservation won over common sense.

'Then follow me.'

'Are you going to be cruel to me again?'

Since his sister's marriage, Lance had spent his life trying to live without any more regret or self-recrimination. Now, Sara's words cut through him, jagged and deep, representing one of his greatest shames. He'd hurt her, calculatedly, deliberately. He'd played on her insecurities and fears in a misplaced desire to protect her from himself. At the time, it had held a twisted kind of logic. Then she'd walked out of his house with her head held high, like the Queen she had once been destined to become, leaving behind her engagement ring, her clothes, and a perfectly pressed handkerchief embroidered with his initials on his bedside table...

It was the handkerchief that had almost undone his resolve in that moment. The realisation that she'd kept it with her since the wake, like something precious. A memory of him. Still, in the days after she'd left, he'd kidded himself into believing that what he'd done had been in her best interests. It was only much later that he'd come to realise he was as bad as her family or Ferdinand, because he'd not given her a choice. He'd taken it from her in a moment of breathtaking arrogance and paternalism, treating her as if she were a child, and not an adult woman who could make decisions for herself about what she wanted in life. Even worse, he'd done it because he was a coward.

The mere fact that she was still willing to speak with him now showed a graciousness he wanted to deserve.

'Was finding me today a chance, or deliberate?' she asked.

He could lie, but truth was all he had left, even though it exposed him. He'd tortured himself over the past months, agonising over Sara's wellbeing. Whether she was safe from the machinations of her family. Whether she was doing well. In the end, appraisal of unwanted items from the Lauritanian royal collection had given him an excuse to be back in the country, and being back in the palace where she worked had made it easy to find out what time her shift finished today…

'Entirely deliberate.'

She sighed. 'Well, that's something, I guess.'

Good or bad, he couldn't be sure, when the full extent of the truth was that he'd been unable to stay away.

Lance followed her like a man being led to his doom, but the barest hope of reprieve kept him putting one foot in front of the other. Even now, she was like a beacon, with her golden hair vibrant in the dim lane ahead of him, wearing a coat the same vivid blue as Lake Morenburg. She had always been the light in his darkest places. Only he hadn't realised it till he'd forced her away and all the light had simply been snuffed out.

He'd learned then how much he loathed the darkness.

They stopped at the door of one of the stone terraces for which the old town was famed. She looked over her shoulder at him, her teeth grazing her lower lip. 'This leads to my apartment. I hope that'll do.'

He'd been desperate to see what she'd made of her life. Rafe and Annalise had been his only means of answering that question, and they'd been naturally protective, telling him little other than confirming that Sara had a job in the palace, curating the art collection, and a place to live.

'I'm humbled you'd have me in your home.'

She hesitated as they reached the top of a narrow flight of stairs, as if about to say something before thinking better of it. Then she unlocked another door to a beautiful airy loft. She walked through the door, inviting him in. The whole space was light and bright, with mismatched rugs on the floor and decorated with well-worn antiques she'd clearly found in the markets below.

'It's not like you're some villain in a dark fairy tale,' she said.

'There I might beg to differ.'

'And that sums up the entire problem.'

She stood in front of windows overlooking the town and the soaring Alps in the distance, every move stiff and weary. He'd done that to her, taken this beautiful, open woman, whose life should be one filled with joy, and somehow left her closed-off and shattered. Of all the things he needed to atone for, this sin was one of his greatest. It started now with his deepest truth. He loved her, to the nucleus of every cell in his body. A sensation so marrow-deep it radiated within him and there was no turning back from it. The heart he'd thought withered, cold and dead could beat again, because she'd shocked it to life.

'You redeemed me, Sara. That was a sin I found hard to forgive when I'd spent so much of my adult life fighting against any kind of salvation. Especially after Victoria.'

The heating in the loft was warm. Sara slipped off her coat and moved to an armchair, draping her coat over it. She gripped the back, fingers digging into the fabric.

'How…is she?'

'She seems to be doing better.'

It had taken six weeks of fighting to be allowed to see Vic in the clinic. He'd gone there to tell her two things. News that he'd ensured the safety of her animals, and news of his broken engagement to Sara. For the first, she'd closed herself in the bedroom of her small suite and came out again ten minutes later seemingly composed, yet with her eyes red-rimmed. As for the second...

'I'm sick of people martyring themselves over me. I refuse to allow you to be another.'

She'd said plenty of other things too, like how he was a fool to pass up a chance of love, and she wouldn't be responsible for his future unhappiness. All whilst hugging him like the warm, adoring young woman she'd once been.

He'd recognised then that he'd given Victoria no agency to help herself, trying to fix things rather than supporting her decisions—good or bad. Perhaps one day she'd tell him what her husband held over her. Perhaps not. For now, he'd done what he could to ensure she was safe, that she had options. She didn't need his guilt. What Vic needed was his love and unquestioning support because his guilt made her trauma about *him*.

Just as with Sara. It had never been about her in the end. He hoped to change that today. If not, he'd walk away only half a person and try once again to live with the sins of his past.

'I'm happy for you and for her.'

He shook his head. 'All this time I'd convinced myself I hadn't saved her. It directed my actions every day. Then you walked into my life, and I knew I had to save *you* or I'd never forgive myself. Yet I was terrified I'd fail and let down yet another person who'd become vital to me.'

Sara's eyes widened a fraction. 'I don't think I was the one who needed saving.'

She was right in every way.

'You and my sister are some of the wisest women I know. And I'm a fool.'

She released the back of the chair she'd been crushing in her hands and turned to look at the view, framed by the soaring mountains in the distance. Her shoulders lifted and fell.

'What do you want, Lance?'

He'd tried living life as the worst version of himself and, in doing so, the cursed memory of his father always won. No more. He raked his hands through his hair.

'I'm trying to make amends. Another fool made you doubt your ability to be Queen here, and yet you *are* a queen because you rule my whole heart. You always will.'

She couldn't look at him, *wouldn't*. If she did, she'd likely run into his arms and never want to leave them, when there was more to be said.

Time and tears had taught Sara many things. Her own value, her own strength, and that she was deserving of love. She'd promised herself when she'd left Astill Hall that she'd only look ahead, and now she needed to clear away that past to make sure she could build the future she craved.

'It was only sex, you said.'

A long exhale hissed in the burgeoning silence between them.

'For a man who prided himself in dealing brutal truths, I told the most terrible lies. When we were together, you reached in and grabbed my soul. I had *never* experienced anything similar. It wasn't sex, it was a connection so intense it consumed me. I was terrified I couldn't protect you. That I'd end up hurting you, yet that's what I did anyway. For that, I can't forgive myself.'

'Of all the things you said, that's what cut the deepest.'

Sara bit into her lower lip. Outside, the sun broke over the mountains and their snow caps gleamed a fierce, blinding white. A tingle at the back of her neck, that sixth sense always attuned to him, told her Lance was closer than before.

'What I should have said is that I love you, Sara. I don't want to slay dragons for you, I'll trap them and train them and have them lie at your feet. The food on my plate, the air that I breathe, it's all ash. I forced you away, and the colour in my life leached to grey.'

A slide of warmth drifted down her spine. The heat of another body standing close behind her. She shut her eyes, absorbing the pleasure of it, swaying back till she bumped against a hard chest. She couldn't move away, not now. She leaned into him and Lance wrapped his arms round her, holding her tight. Right back where she belonged.

'Say something, *please*.' Lance's voice was low and gentle.

'I think…that I'm not the only one who needs their dragons tamed.'

'I hate to admit it, but you're right. Are you offering to carry out that task? If so, I think you'd look rather fetching in armour, wielding a sword. Both of which I could supply from Astill Hall's armoury if you were so inclined…'

She couldn't help the laugh which broke free. Lance had the uncanny ability to fill her life with joy and fun. His arms round her waist squeezed tighter for a second. The weight of his chin rested on her head.

'You have no idea how I've longed to hear that sound again.'

'There hasn't been much laughter for me recently.'

'Let's change that, shall we?'

He loosened his grip on her, gently turned her round and cupped her jaw in his hands. Only now she noticed the bruised quality under his eyes. How the lines of his face had etched deeper. She guessed there hadn't been much laughter for him either.

'Sara, I asked once to be your fake fiancé, but what I want is real and true and permanent.'

Her heart fluttered like a butterfly caught behind her ribs.

'What are you saying?'

'I'm offering you my heart and my soul, if you'll have them. My love and adoration, from today and for as long as I have breath in my body. A ring on your finger and a big wedding if you wish, and if not I don't care. I want you to be mine and me, yours. And some time in the future I hope for little cherubs with blue eyes and golden curls like their magnificent mother.'

The nursery. She knew it. He *had* wanted her to decide. Wanted it as much as she had on that day.

'What if those cherubs take after you?' she asked.

Lance dropped his hands from her cheeks and rubbed one over his face, chuckling. 'Then they'll be little devils and I'll love them all the same. But if you don't love me now, then feel free to reject me as cruelly as I did you. It really is nothing less than I deserve, being the Disappointing Duke, as you so aptly named me.'

Somehow, that title didn't fit any more. It probably never had. She could think of so many more adjectives to describe him, if only he'd believe them himself.

'Do you think you deserve my love in return for yours?'

He hesitated, blew out a slow breath.

'With you, I can achieve anything. It's time to let go of a past that's bound me for too long, and to forge our lives together. Being the best man I can be.'

The last flurry of reserve melted away like the snow in spring. All that bloomed inside her was love and certainty of a future that lay bright and beautiful before her.

'Then you *are* a fool.'

He cocked an eyebrow, the corner of his mouth curving in a wry grin. 'If playing the jester will make you smile, then I'm a fool every day for you. Never doubt it.'

'You're a fool because you've always been the best man for me. My whole problem was that I never *stopped* loving you. Wanting you.'

'I see no problem at all. And you'll have me. Always.'

She put her hand to his chest, the warmth of him pulsing through her. 'My Dashing Duke.'

'Devoted is a better description.' Lance smiled as he bent down and brushed his lips over hers. She sighed when he pulled away too soon, craving more. Craving *everything*.

'If you're going to be the most Delectable Duchess of Bedmore you should probably have the As-till Amethyst.'

'I'm thinking "Disobedient" sounds better. I don't much like the idea of doing what I should. And I hate purple. But I do *love* opals.'

'Whatever you want to be, you're perfect.' Lance reached into his pocket, brought out a small velvet box and opened it. 'Luckily I have this.'

In the afternoon light the old diamonds sparkled. The opal itself, full of fire. He took her left hand in his own and slid the ring onto her finger.

'There, back in its rightful place.'

'My rightful place is with you.'

He sank to his knees. The look on his face was so full of adoration she almost dropped to the floor with him as her legs could barely hold her upright.

'Let's see what we can do about that then. Angel, will you give me the immeasurable honour of becoming my real fiancée, and wife as soon as we can humanly arrange it?'

'Yes, now and for ever.' She smiled, her heart so full of joy and love she thought she might never see a sad day again. 'There's no one else I'd rather be.'

* * * * *